REVIVAL

OF

LOVE

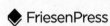 FriesenPress

Suite 300 - 990 Fort St
Victoria, BC, V8V 3K2
Canada

www.friesenpress.com

ISBN
978-1-5255-1524-8 (Hardcover)
978-1-5255-1525-5 (Paperback)
978-1-5255-1526-2 (eBook)

1. FICTION, ROMANCE

Distributed to the trade by The Ingram Book Company

REVIVAL
OF
LOVE

E.P. STASZ

Chapter 1

THE OCEAN WAS RELENTLESS, CONSTANTLY SMASHING ITS waves against the rocks and shoreline. It dazzled with the bright moon dancing on it. She came often, as though the action called to her to come and view its power and beauty. She communed with the Spirits, asking for enlightenment. Coyotes came from the forest twenty feet from her, running along the shore then disappearing around the bend. Owls hooted, but were not sighted. Three deer came to drink at the creek bubbling from between rocks. They kept alert for predators, ears twitched and heads raised as they gazed around, then drank some more. Just as silently, they vanished back into the rocks and trees.

Eventually sleepiness claimed her. Placing the camera and sketchbooks into her bag, homeward she went. Checking her watch, a smile erupted as she realized her research time had increased by two hours. It was midnight.

In her loft apartment she ate lightly, sipped some water then sat, musing. Soon she gathered her supplies and started painting. Quick brushstrokes were interspersed with sips of water. Using the deep colors of the ocean—black, grays, blues, greens, silver with touches of sun on the wave tips—she worked as though guided by unseen forces. Near the break of dawn, she stood and perused the three canvases. Sighing, she signed them, A.L. Waters. She cleaned the equipment and went to bed, lying on top of the covers and quickly drifting into sleep and dreamland.

She was awakened by a buzzing. She finally identified it as the telephone and groped for the receiver. Sasha's cheery voice chased away her sleepy fog. "Wake up, Sister, it's two in the afternoon and birds are singing, people are working for a living and enjoying New York. Belle Wolfe wants more of your work. I'll come by in an hour. Over and out, dear Kate."

Kate scrambled to her feet and quickly showered and dressed. Her mind demanded food: *Eat! Eat!* Checking the fridge, she found fixings for an omelette loaded with nutritious goodies.

Yum. Wonderful food, yes it is. Leaving the area clean, she began to select and ready the week-old paintings for Wolfe. She again blessed them to bring happiness and health to the buyers and viewers.. The Sister transport arrived and they set off to deliver this latest batch of paintings.

Uncovering the canvases at the back of Belle's Art Gallery, both waited expectantly for comments. Months ago, Kate and Belle had met at an artist estate sale. Both were after the empty picture frames bundled into groups. A mutual acquaintance, an ambitious estate handler named Marcy, had invited both Belle and Kate to the sale, where she more or less threw them together: "You seem like strangers but you could be partners, since your work is similar. Belle, meet Kate, painter of marvellous scenes. Belle has an art gallery. Get to know each other."

Belle inquired, "What medium do you favour?"

"Oil. Let me buy these frames and we can discuss over coffee elsewhere."

"Select what you want, then I'd like to learn more about you."

"Here's my card. Why don't we meet at my place? I'll be back there in one hour."

"Kate, take my card. See you soon."

Kate asked the roaming clerk for help to carry her frame selections. Driving away, she wondered if Belle would prove good for her or greedy? Was her gallery well known? Who were the clients? She would concentrate on Belle's aura later, for the deciding factor. Back at her loft, Kate Googled Belle's Art Gallery. She was pleased with the findings.

Belle used her phone to Google Kate, but couldn't make sense of the results. Confused, she sought out Marcy.

"Marcy, Kate gave me her card but look what Google has. Are you tricking me?"

"Heavens no, Belle. Kate uses A.L. Waters to sign her work. She's got talent and unique perspective."

"Oh. Oh. This sample is brilliant. It will be fun to see her work station!"

"What? You are going to her loft?"

"She invited me. Yes I'm going."

"Good. I knew you both had to meet, but I've been so busy. Kate and I met back in college."

*   *   *

"These are magnificent, A.L.!" Wolfe exclaimed. " Each delivery is even better then the last. You must have angels helping. There have been several clients seeking your work. I finally called

Sasha when I couldn't reach you. Step into the office for refreshments and I'll show Jeff where to display them."

A.L. and Sasha were munching on cheese and fruit when Wolfe returned. She took a gulp of coffee and asked, "Costs? For the nine paintings, it's five thousand for you."

"I believe it should be seven for me," stated A.L. "And in the future, will you provide the transport here?"

"I could do the transport if you come during the week they are displayed? Here is my portfolio of all the paintings you offered me. I'll continue keeping tabs, because someday soon by the requests I'm receiving, your fame will be exposed in all its glory."

"Thanks for the portfolio, but I don't need it—I have my own tracking." A.L. considered Wolfe's offer briefly, then shook her head. "Forget about the transport then. I don't flaunt myself. The seven is firm and final."

"If I get more in negotiations/auction?"

"If your fee is out and it's still worthwhile for me, yes! I like to offer funds to the shelters."

Wolfe smiled as she brought out her cheque book, saying, "It's always a pleasure to see what togs you wear. I'll be silent on this new disguise." She hands the payment to A.L..

"Thanks, Wolfe! Your remarkable name captures images for me!"

*   *   *

Sasha and Kate had been friends since college days. While they met studying art, Kate. also studied design, marketing, and some law. Not real sisters, they nevertheless made a good team. Kate was petite, with a swimmer's body, long -ashed blue-green elfin eyes, a pert nose, and a ready smiling mouth. Sasha was a slim and quick-moving brunette with chocolate eyes and a care-free attitude. Today her dark hair was tied in a purple ribbon, to go with her purple caftan and big gold hoop earrings.

At Kate's loft, the girls changed into their regular clothes then addressed lunch. Sasha made a salad of mixed greens, peaches and mushrooms while Kate grilled chicken breasts. They had just begun eating and were reviewing their plans for the coming weekend when they were interrupted by the door-bell ringing steadily.

Kate rushed to open the door for one of their friends, Randal the photographer. He grabbed Kate and swung her in a circle.

"Got some grub for this friend, Kate my girl?"

"Sure. Give Sasha and me the latest news of your exploits."

He hugs Sasha, whispering, "Sasha, girl. How have you been doing with the hairdressing?"

"I like it. Talk later."

Unknown to Kate, Sasha had been doing some training with a hairstylist who needed help. She found it interesting and thought it might be a better fit for her painting, allowing her to use her creativity and meet many different people.

"I," Randall announced grandly, "have received payment from three magazines, where I sent photos and script. Pleased I am. I'll be flying to Toronto for another gig next Tuesday. What have you sold lately?"

"Kate has good news too," Sasha assured him.

"Randal, did you try my idea of the travel agent offices? Yes, I sold some paintings for a neat sum."

"Should I change my career?" Randal turned to Sasha. "And what about you?"

"Come on, Randal," Sasha said. "Everyone has his own feet to stand on. I want to first see that my ideas work. Although my savings are nearly gone. Drat!"

"Sister, just raise the prices on your work and see what happens," suggested Kate. "Randal, do you keep in contact with friends from high school? I received an invite from mine last week but can't make the time to go. I mean to call some girls who live in town but haven't yet. They are married and having kids already!"

"Kate, you are too serious. Some girls marry right out of high school. Look how many were pregnant and still in school. I think they missed out on experiencing life," said Randall. "I had my eye on a gorgeous girl at that time—but others told me she was looking for an out with her family. That made me stay clear of her." He stopped to eat more sandwich. "Man, these sandwiches could be sold at vendors and you would make a killing! They are always unique, tasty, and keep me guessing at the ingredients... Anyway, I'm not tracking old buddies. We chance meet, have a conversation but no exchange of phone numbers."

"What's Adam up to, or have you seen him lately?" Sasha asked.

"I saw Adam last week. He was having a problem with one trainer and released him to the wilds. But he seemed settled. He has a new girl! She dances and does striptease at the Shaw club. She has the physique of a body builder. She evens smells good."

"No way!" Sasha laughed.

"Ha, ha. Gotcha! Really, she is all I said. Well sisters, I'll just be on my way. Thanks for the food. Saturday morning we will brunch together, then take you girls to the carnival."

"The way to the heart is through the stomach. That's why woman feeds man," joked Kate. "We would be delighted to go to the carnival. Be here at ten."

As Randal and Sasha left, Kate wondered about Sasha, since Kate gave her a percentage of her own sales whenever she drove her to the gallery. She went for a run—her usual three to five miles—and returned refreshed and ready to work. She began by scanning the previous night's photos. She selected one and went to the canvas waiting for painting, the floor cloth already spread beneath the easel. She taped an oval frame to exclude paint, then washed lavender over all the canvas. As she began to paint, a sun peeking through clouds, and a rainbow disappearing into them, appeared. Framing this with bold green and black evergreens, she filled in the middle with a river gushing over rocks between rocky banks. A snake is crawled though shrubs by the rock and a squirrel basked in the sun. In the upper tree, she dabbed in a nest with a bird feeding her young.

Kate removed the taped outline from the frame and drank water while she examined her results. Then she continued to paint beyond the frame edge, adding evergreens rising upward on the left and one to bend over the river. She hummed as she painted. Stepping back once more, she scanned her work. Looking at the photo that gave inspiration, she chuckled. She signed the painting in the lower right corner, A.L. Waters. Looking over her paintings from the night before, she was satisfied they were flowing with detail and interest.

It was time to clean the equipment and run again.

She was just lacing up her trainer when the doorbell rang.

Her friend Cora was revealed as Kate opened the door. "How good to see you, Cora. Where have you been hiding? Come in, let's share news."

"Kate, you're a lifesaver! Things are crazy at work. My boss Harold wants me to transfer to the Pittsburgh office for an executive position."

"Girl, that's a promotion! The company should pay for travel and the shipping of your apartment goods."

"Kate. I'm twenty-five and need a partner. I'll be starting from scratch if I take the offer."

"Cora, have you been dating much lately?"

"Four guys had my attention. Alas, none are worthy."

"Take this new offer. You will have other opportunities there. Here, have a juice and sandwich. You've lost weight, girl! Was it intentional or from stress?"

" Umm. Great sandwich! I intended it, then things got crazy at work. I never lost too much. When your man comes along, Kate, will you have me as a bridesmaid?"

"Absolutely, Cora." They sat quietly together as Cora ate, then Kate mused, "Sasha seems more flighty now. I think she wants to change her work focus. She hasn't said, but I feel her dissatisfaction."

"How are Randal and Adam?"

"The guys are doing well in their work. We're going out dancing on Friday, and then to the carnival on Saturday. You know how I love dancing! I've been lucky with Belle Wolfe auctioning some of my paintings and camera work. I did back-up training in marketing but so far I've been able to manage just with the painting."

"You're a good person, Kate. You ground me like my late Aunt Freda." Cora looked around hopefully. "Have you any cookies or cake?"

E.P. STASZ

"I'll not spoil your diet plans. Pour more tea. I have a substitute idea." Kate pulled some frozen yogurt out of the freezer and mixed it with fresh sliced peaches and blueberries.

"Try this, Cora. It's what I use. My tummy is more happy and it keeps the weight down."

"It's good. Have you tried other fruits with it"

"Sure, most work. Adding cold cereal, chia seeds or nuts makes it crunch better."

"Hey Kate, can we do fifteen minutes of line dancing right now? It will be some time before we meet again. I've decided I'll go shake up the workers in Pittsburgh."

"Good decision! Your light shines. I'll select some music. We can shake the floor."

Before sleeping, Kate reviewed her day. "I am thankful for my Baha'i faith. It is the anchor for my soul. I allow myself to love purely, generously, without worrying what I will receive. When others need to empty their cup, I can be trusted to be present and listen. Peace is the release of the love of power for the gain of the power of love. Thank you, Lord, for the gifts of courtesy, prayer, diligence, flexibility, purposefulness, love and commitment."

*　*　*

The weekend came too fast for Kate to finish her planned projects. Kate, Sasha, Adam and Randal were now line dancing in Paul's Bar & Dance. The four friends took a break to sip drinks at the crowded bar counter.

"Paul, you should add a food grill. Too much drink and we need taxis," Adam complained, as the bartended wiped his spilled drink.

"Adam, with your build why do you get tipsy so fast? I swear you only had two drinks!"

"Hey, I can't help it that two other girls on the floor made me taste theirs. They were regulars at my club. I couldn't refuse."

"Kate, see that Adam is not driving tonight," said Paul. "You're the only sane person I can trust here. What have you been painting lately? I need to see more of you."

"I went to Yellowstone Park in Wyoming. The Alberta government in Canada offered them wolves to balance nature. I got shots of the wolves and buffalo. The store there requested the paintings I make using them. I need to work rather than party – but I love to dance so…" Kate looked at the bartender and smiled. "You know Adam's right about adding food. Keep it simple—-wings, soup, sandwiches."

Paul's employee, Carl, came to work the bar and give Paul a break.

Paul took Kate's her hand "Kate. Let's shake the dance floor!"

"Great! Dance I will, partner." Kate jumped up and they made their way through the crowd. There was a tango playing and they stepped into it, laughing. The band gave no mercy and kept playing nonstop, and Paul and Kate stayed on the floor until the end of the set.

"We need a fifteen-minute break, and so do you!" the band leader announced into the mike. "Good to see so many loving the old country favourites along with line dancing!"

Chapter 2

SIX WEEKS LATER, KATE WAS SPENDING AN AFTERNOON AT A new spot on a rocky beach. She had noted before that this beach was not much used by other people. It was beautiful to her. For a while she idly tossed stones into the water to watch the ripples. When the wind became stronger and stirred up the water, she took her her windbreaker from her backpack, stashed the pack by a tall tree near a large boulder, and set to running the shore.

Plucking a water bottle from her stashed pack, she drank deeply and crunched on an apple. Then she was ready to work. Focusing her mind on the contrasts and composition, she started shooting. Sometime later she saw, in the distance, a human walking on the shore. Turning to the other direction, she continued shooting. When the film ran out, she climbed the bank, looking around as she changed film.

Kate desired to be alone when in the creative mood for her shooting and painting. She gathered her gear and walked away from the rocky beach. Back in her car, she drove along the twisty road and came to a mobile food truck. Slipping out of the car, camera on her shoulder, she sought to speak with the vendor about the area and shoot pictures. Clients keep coming with food orders, delaying her chance. Kate sat at a picnic table and zeroed in on the feasting people. Laughing, she caught several in humorous poses, as they shared the different foods.

A stocky senior man with curly white hair approached her table. He wore a gold shirt with khaki slacks and held the hand of a girl about eight years old, in matching yellow T-shirt and shorts. She was busy licking a strawberry ice cream cone.

"Miss, you are an image. Hello, I'm Fred Nader and this is my granddaughter, Lucy. You can take our pictures – but must give me copies." He stretched out his arm to shake hands, and Kate accepted with a soft laugh.

"Pleased to meet you, Fred Nader and Lucy. I'm Kate Knight. I enjoy doing photography. Look at the interesting faces around us!" She looked them over. "I'd love to photograph you. Don't pose though, just play around and have fun together."

Kate stepped back a few feet and started snapping, encouraging them to be silly together and laughing with them as they rubbed noses, shook fists at each other, linked arms at the elbows and danced in place, winked and threw their heads back roaring in laughter.

Seeing the ice cream was melting, Kate said, "Enough! Let's let Lucy rescue her cone. Let me show you what actors you are!"

Fred looked in Kate's viewfinder. "These are wonderful. Dear child, you are finally smiling. Keep it up! Miss Kate, here is my business card. Do send me copies, please." In a lower voice, he explained, "Her mother was an only child and is gone to Heaven. My wife died four months ago."

"I am sorry for all your loss, Fred and Lucy. It will be a pleasure to send you these pictures. Let me give you my business card too. I enjoyed this, thanks."

Fred glanced at the card and gave a surprised smile. "Kate, I am in building construction and you live in one of my properties! How do you like it?"

"My loft is fantastic for the sunlight and the good night lighting, besides having the expansive space I really need for my painting. During the day I'm usually outdoors. Being out in nature makes me feel calm and balanced."

Lucy broke in shyly. "Do you have other pictures besides us in the camera? I want to see them."

Kate opened her digital camera and watched Lucy's face as she viewed coyotes, deer, soccer kids in a pile, a farmer working on repairing a wire fence, and the a group of children with caps on their heads in a hospital room, holding their beautiful drawings.

"I would like to visit these sick children, Grandpa."

"We can arrange that, dear Lucy."

"The best time to visit is ten in the morning," suggested Kate. "Between two and four the day is hard to get through. I mostly go then."

"Well, this was a great day so far. Thanks, Miss Kate. Lucy, how about the zoo trip now?"

"Yes, Grandpa. Thank you, Miss Kate."

Kate bendt to Lucy, saying, "Give me a hug, sweet girl, and I'll see you soon." They hugged, and Kate winked at Fred.

When Kate got home, she took the Nader family photos and printed them as originals, opened the files in Photoshop and played with the backgrounds. She placed a police car behind the image with their fists shaking, had parrots winking at each other behind them, placed a forest with a waterfall behind them dancing and for the laughing shot she put varied flavours of ice cream in buckets on the table. The shot of them rubbing noses took the most manipulation, as she placed icebergs behind them and added a red blanket with fur trim under them. She laughed at herself for being so mischievous. She called Fed Ex to collect them, and faxed Fred Nader a message.

*   *   *

A week later, Kate returned to the new beach in the evening to capture the sky in its glory. Immersed in her camera, she suddenly noticed the sun had faded. Her focus was on the changing color and texture contrasts. Taking a deep breath, she surveyed the forest behind her. A storm was brewing as the wind swept in, changing directions and odours.

She returned to her backpack and stashed her camera. Slipping on the backpack, she turned and saw a man in the near distance looking her way. He started walking toward her and her eyes got bigger. She breathed in his vision. She felt an invisible thread joining them. She was frozen in place. He was her dream vision!

He wore jeans and a T-shirt, with slip-on deck shoes. His curly black hair came to just below his ear. His face was sculpted, strong, tanned and revealed a wide smile. As he came near, he chuckled and said, "A storm will soak us soon if we don't get out of here. Have you a ride close by?" He was studying her face— the stormy eyes, green with golden sparkles, the rosy skin and gorgeous mahogany hair.

She shook her head.

He took her hand and sparks flew though her arm. She jerked her hand, but he held tighter. "Don't be frightened. Did you feel sparks at our touching? Me too! Why don't we go for a coffee up the road?" He led the way as he talked.

E.P. STASZ

In the nearby cafe, at a secluded corner table, they ate chicken burgers, green salad and chocolate cake. He was Todd, she was Kate.

He eyed Kate, asking, "Is photography your career, Kate?"

"I have a lot of interests, though focused on oil painting and photography. I love gardening. I have a passion for my work, but selling art can be problematic so I studied marketing and some law." Kate Eyed Todd and laughed. "Though when I was young I wanted to be a detective. Look where it ended!"

Todd smiled. "That's funny, I'm a lawyer – and I've had thoughts of operating an investigative business! Right now it's in the background. I'm deeply involved in the work at my firm, Hardy, Hanson, Kendel and Denver, near Stanley College. Changing topics… do you dance? Prefer fancy restaurants or simple food? Horror movies or romance? Would you run for politics?"

The time flew by and they laughed and talked together, oblivious to the other patrons. Outside the storm broke tree limbs, poured rainwater dangerously down the spouts and street drains. It went unnoticed by the pair. When the cafe closed at midnight, the storm had moved on. Todd drove Kate to her loft home. He walked her to the door and pulled her against his strong body. He hugged her tightly, then lightly kissed her and again hugged her close for long moments before leaving.

* * *

Todd wanted to leap and shout for joy at having found Kate. His heart was in her hands. He had to leave quickly or his control would snap and he would ravage her. At 36, he had found his soul mate by listening to the emotions surfacing when he studied his purchased paintings.

Kate, meanwhile, looked at her current paintings and noted the face emerging from the mist. In another it was shielded with leaves like camouflage. The face was similar to Todd's. He was so handsome and comfortable in openly discussing his life. She was thirty and should know her heart, but did she?

They met every evening after his office hours to learn more of each other.

Todd looked into Kate's beautiful eyes as they shared their family stories. "I have an older sister living in Spain with her chef husband. Our parents travelled, doing archaeology digs in different countries. They were killed ten years ago in Ethiopia when their camp was overrun by opposing political militia. Tell me about your family."

"Todd, I'm sorry for your loss. I have two older brothers. They taught me sports. Brian is in house construction and Mark is a pharmacist. They expect me to call if I ever need help. My mom lost the battle with cancer soon after I graduated university. She was a wonderful mom, wife, friend, and neighbour. She had a talent for cooking, sewing and gardening. Dad too has passed. We lived on a farm in Alberta, but Dad had a restless nature and also did trucking."

"What sports interest you, Kate?"

"Dancing, tennis, baseball, volleyball, dancing, bowling, curling, swimming and dancing."

"You really like dancing! We match. I still do most of those. Who are your close friends?"

"You could meet some on Friday. Hudson's at seven—we can partner in tennis with Sasha and Adam. Can you make it?"

"I'll enjoy meeting them. But not it's late, and I have court tomorrow. I'll take you home now."

The next days passed in a whirl. They joined the other at the bowling alley and had a fun time. They went dancing at Jake's Slip & Slide, laughing through the night. They ran track, played tennis, and took toys for the NYC Graham Children's Hospital Foundation. Kate was obsessed with him. Home alone, she frantically painted every evening until near dawn. She hardly slept, yet was energized.

One month after their first meeting they walked the shore, ending with a light meal. After another hour of talking, he invited her to come home with him. He parked in a garage that also held a green motorcycle. His home, thought Kate, looked big enough to fit six of her lofts. Inside, they toed off their boots and she dropped her backpack on padded bench in the front hall. Todd took Kate's hand, still feeling energy sparks at the touch, and embraced her. He led her to the living room and stopped before a painting of crashing waves in blues, greens, purples, and greys, offset by the sun peeking through the turbulent clouds. She was startled but pleased to see it was one of hers. Its colors were repeated in his room accessories. He turned her to face him and kissed her.

"I have seen you at the shore many times," he said. "There was a force demanding that I go to that place. I couldn't wait any longer to contact you. Come with me."

He led her into his bedroom. This room had a blue-black decor with dashes of yellow, with gems held in a large ornate dish. He smothered her in kisses, on her eyes, then all over her face and murmured, "My love, my one and only." His teeth lightly bite her bottom lip and he tongued her mouth. She was all honey sweetness and a hint of raspberry.

She was swooning. The joy, to be kissed like this by him! She drew a deep breath. She stroked his back and arms, feeling his warm muscles at his shoulders and the leanness of his waist. His woodsy scent enveloped her. Her body yearned and blushed under his touch. He opened her blouse, unclasped the lacy blue bra, then captured her breasts in his hands. He swirled his thumbs on her nipples, lightly pinching the ends until they hardened like diamonds. Soon his head was down and he was kissing and swirling his tongue on them.

"I need you. Let me love you, Kate."

The passion swept over and through her. She had to feel his skin next to her and flung his shirt sideways, ripping the buttons and sending them flying. Soon he had her jeans off and held her away from him to admire her. "Lovely, lovely Kate. So soft and rose-scented—I yearn for you!" He placed her on the bed and dropped his shirt and jeans, then lay beside her. His hands travelled her length, exciting her all the while he was kissing her thighs, tummy, returning to her throat, ears, eyes then mouth. She moaned as he explored her body. She was steeped in pleasure. Her pulse was erratic. He slipped her panties off.

She felt his hand on her cleft and drew a quivering breath. She was wet and his skin was damp. He perspired, trying to hold himself in check until she was satisfied. Still kissing, he gently worked his hand through her lower mound hair to the tender flesh, circling to awaken the nerve endings. He hooked two fingers within and moved upward, pressing to find the sensitive swollen place just inside. She moaned and rose to him.

"You're awesome, Kate. So hot and so tight. You're my sweetheart." Her orgasm bloomed and she shouted his name, then lay shaking uncontrollably. She was surrounded in dazzling, awesome Northern lights.

"Todd, you're amazing! You overwhelm me. I was never loved before."

He nudged his knee to spread her legs and gently started to ease into her. She gasped. Perfect ! She was his, only his! He hesitated, studying her face for moments, continuing to kiss her and she eagerly responded. She clenched his back. He carefully eased in and out, going a little deeper each time until she tightened around him. She wrapped her legs around him and they rocked in blissful passion. They loved each other fully and deeply, as nature intended. They rolled, keeping their love flowing and tangling the sheets. Finally they lay sated. He felt exalted. They mated many times this first night together.

It was Saturday. Todd held his love close as they woke in his bed. Kate's head was on his chest and she moved, stretched and groaned Her mind reeled from what she has done! *Where is my self-respect now? I must consider what choices remain.*

"Sweet Kate, my love, I'm yours and you are mine!" Todd brought her body tight to his again. She kissed him, then wiggled away, saying, "I've had a loving workout with you, Todd. Now we need food and movement outdoors. Up now. No more loafing in bed." Swinging her legs over the bed edge she stood and streteched. Looking back at him, she coaxed him with her finger to follow, as she searched for the shower room. "Start the water, I'll be back quickly. I need something from my pack."

She was soon back with her special soap. "Todd, do you like the water hot like I do?" She stepped gingerly into the shower.

"We are on the same wavelength, beautiful Kate." He took the soap and lathered it, covering her body slowly from neck to her toes.

Kate pushed him against the wall and rubbed her body against his, then took the soap and covered him thoroughly. "Time to rinse!"

"Not so fast Kate, I need to feel you." The water streamed over them as they loved each other once again.

Eventually they got around to shampooing their hair.

"Kate, what ingredients are in this soap? It feels and smells like the forests."

"I have a friend who makes it for me. She had bad eczema and developed herbal products to treat and cure it. Now she has herbal mixtures for many uses. It leaves your skin clean without any residue left behind, and it keeps hair strong and shining besides smelling great!"

While she talked, Todd towelled her dry and wrapped her in a lady's robe.

Kate said, "I'll fix you a smoothie, then let's head outdoors— the day is slipping away. We must treasure God's wonders!"

* * *

Later in the day, back in his home, they eat a ham and vegetable omelette. Relaxing on the sofa listening to music, his arm wrapped around her shoulder; Todd states, "I must reveal something to you, Kate."

"I already know you are not a lawyer but a policeman! However I, too, have a secret to reveal, Todd. Should we put our secrets in a short note, and see how close we fit?"

They wrote them and exchanged papers.

She read his aloud: "I love A.L. Waters (alias Kate). My heart and soul belong to Kate. Please marry me."

He softly read hers: "I paint and do photographs. I sell undercover to Belle's Art Gallery. You have some of my paintings. P.S. I love you with my heart and soul."

They looked at each other and started laughing. He hugged her tightly. "See, we fit absolutely. We are heart and soul together. Will you marry me, sweet Kate? I need you."

Kate squirmed. "I too need you, Todd. We should have waited for marriage before making love. I think we should use a Justice of the Peace and do it quietly this week." Her eyes searched his face.

"You would forgo a traditional wedding?"

"Later we must have a Baha'i marriage ceremony. We discussed this before."

"Yes, I remember," said Todd. "I'll find a JP and we'll marry this week."

"Take my ring and delight me with your choice."

"Wait right here, love. I need to fetch something." Todd disappeared into his bedroom. When he returned, he took her left hand and slid a ring—a sapphire surrounded with nine diamonds—onto her fourth finger. "To me it reflects your spirit and eyes, Kate."

"It's splendid, my love." She gazed into his eyes and they embraced.

Chapter 3

FOUR MONTHS LATER THEY HAD A BAHA'I MARRIAGE CER-
emony. Kate's brother Mark and wife Tracy came to support
Kate. The wedding was kept small, with close business associates and friends.

Todd wore a white tuxedo with a sky-blue shirt, blue and
white tie and blue cummerbund. His two best friends, Shane
and Scott, wore grey tuxedos with sky-blue accessories.

Kate's antique ivory satin and lace gown flattered her curves.
Her long veil was decorated with pearls, while sapphires inter-
mingled with pearls adorned her elegant neck and ears. Her two
flirting bridesmaids, Sasha and Cora, wore organza blue-green
gowns with ivory and blue accessories. Lucy, the flower girl,
tossed petals on the walk up the aisle to the join Todd. She wore
a white organza dress with a long blue sash. Her head held a
circlet of blue wrapped with a rope of white organza and pearls.

Kate's brother Mark led her to Todd.

"Todd, you will treasure my sister with love and a long marriage." After hearing Todd's reply—"My heart is committed to
Kate, Mark"—he placed Kate's hand into Todd's,

Baha'i dignitaries and the guests witnessed the couple exchange vows.

The reception was lively, with laughter punctuating the many speeches offered to the couple. The Brothers Band played wonderful dance music, even asking the folks to do some line dancing. Men lined up to do so and brought the house to a roar. Later the ladies lined up, and Mark's wife gave their request to the band. Soon the ladies were tapping moves to "Elvira," and "Gypsy Cowboy." The audience clapped and laughed, then returned to feasting and dancing.

Much later, Fred Nader took Todd and Kate aside. " I am very pleased you found each other. Todd, you had the perfect vision of how your house was to be built. Kate, have you found it so?"

"Wherever Todd will be, so will I. Did you put special secrets inside his home, Fred?"

"Todd will let you know if you cannot discover them. Have a healthy, blissful, prosperous marriage, dear Kate and Todd."

Kate threw her bouquet over the crowd, and it was caught by her friend, Adam. Everyone cheered him. "Man, what am I going to do with all my girlfriends?" Adam joked.

His friends jeered, "You have to make careful selections now, Romeo!"

*   *   *

A helicopter left them at Todd's cabin in the Catskill mountains for their honeymoon week. Kate's eyes scanned over forest, waterfall and cliffs before spotting the red roof and cabin.

"Todd, I was raised in a log cabin with a red metal roof and red door!" Kate chuckled.

Todd's cabin had windows facing east, south and west. There was a covered large deck below all the windows. Todd carried her over the threshold and, setting her feet down, stated, "This is all yours, sweet wife of mine!" He kissed her thoroughly. "Years ago, my parents had this cabin built. I have a company that checks it regularly and stocks groceries when it is to be used."

"It's wonderful, Todd. I adore the vaulted ceiling and the open concept. And all the windows, bringing in the outdoors." Scurrying ahead, she checks a washroom and two bedrooms below, then rushes up the stairs finding a large bathroom, master bedroom and library. She yells, "I love it! I love it!"

Todd followed her up the stairs and grabbed her as she turned to go back, saying, "Come with me, loving wife. Let me ravish you now!" He led her back into their bedroom. She never noticed the big painting facing the bed. It was hers. It had animal faces and a hidden man and woman gazing at each other.

Much later the newlyweds surfaced to bathe and go in search of food.

*   *   *

Through the week they cooked together, moving smooth as a dance. Todd willingly ate Kate's vegetarian choices. They hiked, swam below a waterfall, fished, played cribbage and chess. Mostly, they made love.

Chapter 4

IN THE THREE MONTHS THEY'D BEEN MARRIED, KATE AND Todd had developed their backyard into a lush sanctuary with a waterfall, beautiful trees, vegetable garden, shrubs and perennial flowers. Annual flowers were added as the seasons changed. Friends came by to give some help with the project and then coerced the couple to accompany them to their backyards for a grilled meal. More friends came for these, and expanding the couples' circle of business contacts.

Her brother Mark called, asking her to send some paintings his way. "I bragged about your work and now they want to buy some. Help me, Kate! It's for your benefit too."

"Okay, bro. I'll place price stickers on them, but you must add in the shipping cost and divide it among all the paintings I send. I hope you will let them know my work is unique and in demand."

"Sis, I did let them know. When are Todd and you coming to visit us?"

"We've nearly finished landscaping the back yard. I'll let you know when we can get away. I'll finish some more paintings and you can expect delivery in nine days."

"Love you, little sis. No doubt the parcel will reveal surprises."

"Of course I need to surprise you. Love you back, big bro! See you when we can."

*   *   *

The Yellowstone store needed more of Kate's work. She worked feverishly for two weeks to fulfill the order and ship the paintings. She had received a cheque from her brother for all the parcelled paintings. Friends she grew up with sent her letters, expressing their love of her work and the joy of owning one or more.

Lately, her paintings were showing more vibrant, nearly violent colors. Several were done before she noticed the change. Considering this, she planned to take them to Belle's Gallery as soon as they dried. She cleared up the studio, then focused her mind to review the meditation process that was such an important part of her spiritual life:

Step 1: Use the powerful Faith prayers. Remain in silent contemplation a few minutes.

Step 2: A decision comes forth ? It answers the prayer/ solves the problem.

Step 3: Be determined to carry decision forth

Step 4: Have faith and confidence that the power will flow through you, the right way will appear, the door will open, the right thought, the right message, the right principle, or the right book will be given to you. Have confidence and the right thing will come to your need. Rise from prayer, take the next step.

Step 5: Act as though it has all been answered. Act with tireless, ceaseless energy. As you act, you become a magnet, which will attract more power to your being, until you become a clear channel for Divine power to flow through you.

How true are these words "Greater than the prayer is the spirit in which it is uttered, and greater than the way it is uttered is the spirit in which it is carried out." (Shoghi Effendi, Principles of Baha'i Administration, p. 91)

She went running to keep up her routines, then headed home to shower and change. She called Fed Ex and had her paintings sent to Belle. Todd was off to London, England on his last assignment for Hardy, Hanson, Kendel and Denver. He had landed a new position in Philadelphia, and the couple would be moving. Perhaps, Kate mused, they could soon start a family.

* * *

When the phone rang, Kate was still daydreaming about her art and the changes to come. She was jolted alert by the voice of their friend, Scott Hayes. Scott was an FBI agent and he said quickly, "Kate, I'm afraid this isn't a casual call. Stay home, I'm coming over!"

Kate wondered what he would reveal, alternately intrigued and worried, until the doorbell finally rang.

Agent Hayes took her hand and led her to a kitchen chair. " Sit, Kate."

"Scott, you are scaring me. Did we win a lottery?"

"There is no easy way to say it. Todd has been kidnapped."

Kate sat silent, blank with shock, as the FBI agent filled a glass of water and brought it to her. Finally she found her voice. "No. No. There's no way he's in danger. No. No."

She grabbed the water and drank it down, trying to push down the rising tide of fear.

Scott is put his hand on her shoulder. "I'm sorry Kate. The FBI were informed of a bomb aboard the plane and the flight was cancelled. We got the passengers removed to safety, but unfortunately, somebody got to Todd before the FBI."

"There must be airport cameras that catch foul play. Are they being examined?"

"Yes, for sure. I must warn you—the media will soon have the plane story broadcast. Don't let it frighten you. The FBI are more factual and accurate."

"Why did Todd become a target?"

" Kate, he was working undercover with the FBI."

Biting her lips and studying the agent's face, she whispered, "I know. He said there was little chance of being detected. It was only for a couple weeks!"

"Todd was to supposed to keep it from you— you must be a close couple." The agent sighed. "There were six members of the Mob on board; it's possible they were the target and Todd somehow got in the way. But our concern now is to find him."

Kate was gulping air, trying to marshal her scattered thoughts. "Am I a target now too?" she asked.

"I'm afraid so." The agent was grim. "You knew he was undercover. If the kidnappers find that out, they may see you as a risk."

"So what happens? Will the FBI give me a safe house until they find Todd? But then… they got to Todd before you could save him, so how can I expect safety from the FBI?"

"I've called a B&B security company to come here and place cameras on all sides of the house, the garage and the main drive to catch licence numbers. I know Todd already has a tight alarm for the house."

"Perhaps I should stay with friends or family. No, they could be harmed." A new and unwelcome thought came to her. "Reporters will be here, harassing me. I can't handle that!" A thought occurred to her. "Scott, has the FBI or police used psychics with success?"

"You believe that stuff?!" Hayes took one look at her face and reconsidered. "Sorry, I take that back. I do know of one in Baltimore that helped the police. He goes by S. S. Kelly. He uncovered a baby snatching organization. Want me to call him?"

"Look, your B&B security is at work now." Sure enough, a crew had pulled up and the first camera was being mounted.

"Kate, we aren't sure at this point who kidnapped Todd. It could be the Mob or it could be his legal firm; his investigation involved both."

"Are you tracking all the partners in the firm?"

"Yes, Kate. We're especially interested in Jack Kendel, who formed the legal company, and Lloyd Hardy, his Chief."

Kate was suddenly clear on her course. "Alright, I've decided! I'm going travelling. I'll take tour buses. I have your camouflage techniques and my outfits. I can take photos for my future work. I'll have my cell with me, but I won't use it. You contact my cell when there is information. I'll go pack now." She hurried away, then popped her head back into the kitchen. "Clean out the fridge, will you, and dispose of the contents? Bags are in the pantry."

What a gal! thought Hayes. *Come on, Todd, buddy, get a message to us.* He grabbed the garbage bags and cleared the fridge quickly. He placed them by the B&B truck and asked them to dispose of them, then checked the garage vehicles to confirm their readiness. Back in the kitchen, he tried a call to S.S. Kelly. No answer.

Kate returned dressed in a straw hat, khaki pantsuit and white T-shirt, sunglasses and a determined attitude. She rummaged in the pantry and pulled out survival bars and a couple of water bottles, placing them in a side pocket of her backpack. "Scott, I called the police chief and told him what I'm doing and why. I called security for the house and informed them too. I'll walk a couple blocks, then take a taxi to the bus station. Make it Priority One to find Todd. Nail whoever did this and bring him home safe."

Chapter 5

ARRIVING IN BALTIMORE, KATE SAT IN THE BUS STATION studying the telephone books to find food and S.S. Kelly. She placed the info into her cell phone, then hurried to the street to find the restaurant for a decent meal. In the restroom she refreshed herself with cool wipes on her neck. She devoured the shrimp rice dish and lemon pie without tasting it.

Back on the street, she waved down a taxi and headed to Kelly's home. It was a beautiful log home with large east- and south-facing windows. Asking the taxi driver to wait, she walked to the front door and rang the bell. No answer. Then she walked around the house, finding a beautiful redhead leaving the barn and walking toward her.

Kate called "Hi. I need to see S.S. Kelly. Is that you?"

Laughing, the redhead replied, "No, Lass. I'm Andrea, usually called Andy. Why do you need Kelly?"

"I'm Kate and my business is with Kelly."

"He is my brother and he left a day ago to help someone. I'm looking after his horses. Would you like some tea? Where do you live? Your aura is troubled and your eyes are sad. You need a

tea. Go on in, and I'll drive you where you want to go after this."
Andy went to inform the taxi driver.

He replied, "Lucky you, she paid me up to here. I'll get her bags."

Andy entered the home, dropping Kate's bags by the entry. Kate already had the kettle whistling. She stands holding a cat's eye quartz.

"Quite beautiful, you and the cat's eye. Here's the teapot. Do you take sugar or milk? No? Good."

Kate efficiently made tea and set two cups on the island. "Andy, this is a beautiful home. The cat's eye brings back memories of my Irish grandmother. You read my emotions quickly. What is your gift, Andy?"

"I heal by touching. Have some tea. There must be a cookie of some kind here." Andy rummaged in a cupboard for a minute. "Yes. Here we go." She emerged with an Oreo bag and placed several cookies on a plate. For a few minutes they both drank and ate their cookies in silence.

Andy turned to Kate and took her hands. She bowed her head.

"You are married and he is lost. Kate, take the cat's eye and hold it while you meditate. Sit still and allow the spirit to enter. Act on the message." There are minutes of silence. "Your spirit and creativity are released by closeness to water, forests and animals. You do successful work."

*   *   *

As Andy drove, Kate explained her plan. "I'm taking tour buses to stay away from the trouble in New York. The FBI know how to contact me."

E.P. STASZ

"Kate, it is better for you to fly to settings of forest and water then stay here any longer. I suggest going to the Yellowstone Park in Wyoming. Or for something closer, you can fly to Du Bois, Pennsylvania, then take a tour bus through the scenic Shannon State Forest and beyond. Travel by car south on Highway 30 along the river. There are three campsites along the way. By this time you should feel better and may have FBI news. You decide from there, and my prayers go with you."

"May I have your e-mail address Andy? And could you take me to the closest airport?"

As they travel, Kate repeatedly sang a Baha'i prayer. "Thy name is my healing, O my God, and remembrance of Thee is my remedy. Nearness to Thee is my hope and love for Thee, my companion. Thy mercy to me is my healing and my succour." The familiar, comforting words strengthened her.

Thirty minutes later they arrived not at an airport, but at a farm. Andy explained, "Kate, this man has a private airplane and he can help you." She honked the horn and hopped out to greet her friend. "Phil, we can use your remarkable skills, my friend. Kate needs to go to Du Bois. Will you help?"

"Phil, I can pay you, kind sir."

Phil laughed. "I had a ringing tune in my ear and knew Andy would soon show herself. I checked the plane twenty minutes ago! Kate, I just need to clear my travel route and then we can head out."

Soon they were in the blue skies with a few clouds.

Chapter 6

THE BIG TOUR BUS SLOWED AND SUDDENLY STALLED, coughed and belched blue-black smoke. The driver loudly exclaimed, "HELL! DAMNATION!" He stood and addressed the passengers.

"Sorry folks, another problem besides our guide having to leave us! Next bus will leave at 7:30 am. There is an all-night restaurant a block ahead, and a motel adjacent for those needing sleep. Give the morning driver your receipts and you'll be paid. I'll set out all your baggage from below and have a driver drop them at the motel. Take all your belongings from inside, please."

Kate had been sleeping, and it took her awhile to fully wake up. She looked at her watch—9:30 p.m. Travelling with the tour were several older teens, two families each with three preschool children, and two senior men. She waited for them to exit, slowly collected her backpacks and headed to the restaurant. The teens, she noted, had headed to an arcade and the families to the motel.

Two older men that Kate remembered from the bus were already seated in the restaurant. They nodded at Kate as she came near and chose the only clean booth, across from them. Kate thought they seemed too distinguished to be bus travelling.

The cheery waitress who came to take orders exclaimed, "That bus has broken down twice before! Luck is with you all, as the morning driver has been a very good replacement! I'm Jan, and if anyone's looking for a job, I need a cook or waitress ASAP." She turned to the two older men. "I bet the two wise men want coffees, and specials?"

They nodded, laughing, and she winked at them.

"She's still coddling us, Sam!" joked one, earning a laugh from Jan before she spoke to Kate.

"What is your pleasure, Miss?"

"Mushroom soup, toast and tea, please. Have you a local paper here?"

"I'll bring the paper, then get the orders." Jan swiftly brought the *Seattle Blues* and left for the kitchen. "I bet the Yorks will entice the Miss to disclose personal business. They're like lawyers always searching for new challenges."

While they waited for their order, the fathers of the young children on the bus entered the restaurant, sat on the bar stools near the kitchen and ordered food and drinks to go.

One of the older men caught Kate's eye. "Miss, I'm Sam York and this is my brother Bob. We live in the next town, and run that newspaper you're reading. We leave the office to refresh our perspective, see varied peoples and find news as we travel. We have a total of one hundred and twenty two years of experiences. This tour experience is not what you or we signed for, but we think of it as adventure!"

Jan brought out the orders to the fathers, who paid and headed back to the motel with their take-out.

"I'm travelling and working as I vacation and see the country. My name is Kate Denver." *What the hell! Why did I give my full name?* She put her hand on her mouth, shook her head and closed her eyes, realizing she had to be more alert. Drat, she was so tired.

Singing a ditty, Jan brought their food.

Kate fingered the cat's eye gem in her pocket, then looked toward Sam and Bob. She asked, "Are there any resorts or other outdoor jobs around the area?" Being in jeans, hiking boots and carrying a backpack, they should think she was athletic.

"Sure," Bob offered. "The Red Rock Resort hires trail guides, housekeepers and cooks. They even have a singing bar and separate guest cabins. The family operating it are our friends, Mike and Trudy Farrell. The Resort is near our city. A pretty lady like you will be employed in no time!"

Sam said carefully, "You seem sleepy, and that can make you less cautious than you should be. I recall… are you a relation to the Denver who was kidnapped? Watching Kate closely, he continued more softly. "If so, we'll give you protection. No one else heard you speak here."

She was so tired. *I've got to trust these men, who seem so like my dad. Why didn't I use my alias name? Was I hoping to end my journey? Gad, I'm lame, lame!*

She was too exhausted to keep running. "Okay! I need to see drivers' licenses or passports, to gain my trust!" Bob and Sam dug out their passports and handed them over, chuckling as she copied them into her cell phone.

"Okay!" Kate resigned herself to admit she was that Denver, but first she had one more check to make. "Would you excuse me for a moment?" She left to speak to Jan. Kate asked Jan if she could vouch for the men. Jan said, "Sam and Bob are very generous in philanthropy; my daughter and son benefited with scholarships for their university studies. Many others received financial help and wisdom from them. You better believe you can rely on them! I would have interrupted and taken you into the kitchen, if there was doubt. I'm always watching for potential trouble. Weeks ago a man threatened his partner that he'd drown her if she left him. I called the police. He had warrants issued for his arrest. Yup! They arrested him right here!"

"Thank you, Jan!"

Kate returned to her table, and looking at Sam and Bob, said, "Your one hundred twenty two years must hold much better wisdom than I. How can you help?"

Sam explained they would be like guardians to her. Bob invited her to join forces with them. He thought it would be best to sleep at the motel, and keep separate until they reached the tour stop at Seattle. They would get a driver to inconspicuously bring her to their home. Later, Bob paid their food bills and the Yorks left for the motel. Kate returned to the kitchen and thanked Jan again.

Kate hoped the motel had good locks and plenty of hot water for a soaking bath. As she walked slowly to Brad's Motel, she noted the colors, conditions and kind of autos parked on the streets. Entering her room, she locked the door, placed a chair under the doorknob, and then sat on the bed looking at the surroundings. A small TV sat on a small dresser. Checking the drawers, she found a Bible and a pocket book for reading, but in the last drawer was someone's forgotten Halloween mask. What a miserable housekeeper worked here, she thought. No, probably a teen who had to work fast and escape to be with friends. *Shut up, Self!* She rubbed her head and eyes and went to the bathroom. It had bright yellow walls making it cheerful, with a small window above the tub. She looked in the mirror and started the hot water flowing for a bath.

From her backpack she took a toiletry bag and tilted in some drops of bubble bath soap. She tried to hurry and undress but she was all thumbs. Finally she stepped into the water to soak. She dozed for fifteen minutes, to awaken in cool water. She stood and reached for the towels. Whoa! They were fluffy ones! Joy! She brushed her teeth and wiped the steamed mirror.

She brushed and braided her hair, slipped into a blue T-shirt and yoga pants, crawled between the covers and hoped for sleep. She fell asleep quickly, but her rest was interrupted by dreams of running, explosions, strange faces and places. She twisted and turned back and forth, getting twined into the bedsheets.

She awoke groggy and groaning and got up to use the bathroom. She returned to bed, this time only covering herself lightly with the comforter, but shortly she awoke again all sweaty. Still half asleep, she showered and without drying, returned to bed and lay on top. Finally, she slept.

Chapter 7

NICK FARRELL WAS GUIDING SIX YOUNG EMPLOYEES FROM Portland, Oregon through the twisty varied trail, drawing attention to flora and fauna and the awesome views. "Please note this is Number Four Trail. Whenever you hike a trail, always use a guide, since various wild animals roam this beautiful natural area. Three weeks back, we needed an ambulance for a lone hiker we found. He was dehydrated, bruised and very lost. He was not registered at the resort. Police later informed us that he was a writer with published articles in nature magazines. He had recently lost his wife and child in a plane crash. The bereavement society is counselling him in his home town."

When they stopped for a food break, he treated three ladies for blisters and the others for cuts and scratches. Nick had a sinewy tall figure with deep blue-black hair worn shoulder length, all enclosed in wide smiles, safari hat and witty jokes.

Four hours later, he slipped into the family hot tub and groaned, relishing its soothing pleasure. His sister Beth, about seven months pregnant, came to talk about the hike, wondering which trail was taken and whether the hikers were honest about their fitness level. She dangled her feet in the tub and laughed as she splashed him.

"What the heck, who's the worker?" he shouted. His hand snaked out and pulled her into the tub.

She sputtered, "Don't, don't!"

Their shouting masked the footsteps of Beth's husband Phil, who carried a tray of sandwiches and drinks. "Well, well, brotherly love showing again, Beth? Here's something to strengthen and energize you wet ducks! How was your day, bro? What are you doing about your vacation time?"

"I'm checking with Sam and Bob to see what noteworthy research they need. Mom mentioned they called and wanted my help. Though I really wanted to finish restoring my Mustang, which was placed on the back burner." He gobbled sandwiches and groaned in pleasure. "This tub is a lifesaver after these past months of heavy hiking and carpentry!"

Beth had changed into a dry outfit and sat munching on sandwiches. Phil eyed her and stated that the protein fruit milkshake was her treat. His attention to her diet showed concern and care.

"My squeaky wheel needs grease, guys," Beth said. "Can I go with you, Nick? Then I can visit Mavis and I'll find my own way home."

"That's a great idea, my wife, since I'll be flying to Portland for three days of legal business.," Phil said. Nick said he was happy for the company, and left to check on the Resort guests.

Phil and Beth started discussing his work and why he never told her sooner. "It's not a dramatic case, sweetheart," he said. "I only learned about it this evening. I was wracking my brains trying to find something to interest you while I was away. This trip will solve it." He kissed her passionately. Beth exclaimed, "Admit it! Bro rescued us again!"

*   *   *

The Portland hikers were in the Red Rock Resort guest hot tub, drinking champagne, eating snacks and giggling about the handsome muscled guide, Nick. They had enjoyed the steep, twisty trails that left them hugging some cliff edges. Nick had revealed several awesome, breathtaking God-made vistas. This trip was so much better than working out in a smelly gym and fending off the advances of sweaty guys.

"On tomorrow's agenda," read Sheila, "we kayak with Jim from 10 -3 p.m. It's great that the lodge takes such good care of us—equipment, food, medical all provided. This is the most relaxed vacation I've had."

Cindy piped up, "Three days of activities, and all male guides! How did you do it, Sheila?"

"I know," Nancy teased. "Sheila has a very persuasive way of stating facts at the office. Why not use them here? The boss hasn't found out where we went or she'd already be back at work. And we still have ten days to go."

Lauren was twisting her hands and with an anxious face said, "My sub asked all kinds of questions about my boss, Kirk. Maybe she wants him? That would sure fix his anger at me. If that happens, I'll never request her again! Except… she is the best worker sub we've ever had."

The twins, Jill and Judy, laughed at the others. "Keep worrying instead of relaxing and we'll all be in tears tomorrow!" said Judy. "Fun! Fun! We are here to bust our butts and have Fun! Fun!"

Later the girls dined, then left to power walk though the grounds. Still energized, Jill and Judy encouraged the others to go shopping locally because "sightseeing is better than sitting around."

Everyone laughed and each complimented the twins for keeping them hopping. They borrowed a Jeep from the resort and drove to a shopping district in Seattle, then parked and briskly strolled the sidewalk. They stopped to browse through antique stores, craft shops, a bookstore and a jewellery shop. Lauren and Cindy had bags of purchases. Cindy was delighted with the figurines she found to expand her niece's collection. Lauren loved wearing spike-heel shoes, but they killed her feet. She made a great find of cushy walking socks at the craft place. Sheila had two new authors for bedtime reading. Jill and Judy handed water bottles to the girls.

"Where did we park the Jeep, girls?" Nancy asked. "I'm all turned around !"

"We sure got used to others taking care of us!" stated Sheila.

The others considered and finally figured out where to find the jeep.

Back at the resort, Nancy, looking to each person, proposed, "We should all weigh in and do measurements before turning in tonight. It will be a good comparison three weeks from now!"

So after showering, wearing the bare essentials, they each got weighed, measured and recorded.

Sheila said, "It would be good motivation to give out prizes! Let's have a reward for 1) the most weight loss, 2) the most difference in 'flab' turned to muscle, and 3) the best tan. Have I covered enough?"

Jill and Judy tossed cushions at her and said, "No! No way! We do our own rewards. We want our friendships to last!"

Chapter 8

BOB YORK RESEARCHED THE NEWSPAPER STORIES AND TELE-vision reports for details on the kidnapping. He read that Todd Denver was a NYC prominent lawyer, who had... *Whoa, this is interesting...* and further, his wife had vanished and the *New York Gazette* was offering a reward for information on her. No wonder Kate was running. Sam had noticed her several stops back. The brothers had watched her and decided there was some story in that lonely, tired-looking individual. Her sad blue-green eyes and lovely mouth revealed a beautiful but scared Kate. At times she was witty, asking questions of the tour guide. Sam and Bob knew several FBI agents and Bob decided to contact Matt Neil.

The Yorks had an impressive estate. The grounds were manicured and enhanced with landscaping of varied trees and blooming flowerbeds, but all Kate wished for was a hot bubbly bath and lots of sleep. Seeing this she fell into remembering... Todd had been enthused about changing careers. Hehad such an inquiring mind. He had made connections with an investigative group in Pittsburgh and given his notice at the legal firm. Todd had been on the last London job for his company. Damn! Damn!

Her thoughts were interrupted by someone shaking her shoulders. Refocusing on the now, she heard, "Miss. Miss. Are you alright?"

She shook her head. "Just... just... give me a minute."

Looking up, she saw a concerned butler who said, "Breathe deeply three times! Okay. Do it again. Good! I'll take your bags. I am Alan. Please follow me." He headed up the house steps, looking behind for her. In the foyer he said, "I saw you arrive. The driver said you've had some trouble. It's safe here. Follow me to your room, and Dory will come to assist you. A hot bath will help relieve your aches and stress. The York men are not here yet, but will be back at four."

Dory O' Dell bustled in cheerily, singing some Irish tune, and said in a singsong lilt, "Come Miss, the bath is ready and I'll take your clothes to laundry. Here are toiletries for you. I'll fetch some tea and lunch." Dory stood five-five with an athletic build, and wore quiet running shoes, with lightweight pocketed jeans and a colorful top. Her reddish-brown hair framed a happy round face.

Dory soon returned with a tray of fruit, ham-wrapped cheese and asparagus, scones, a tiny pot of jam and tea. Setting it on a stool next to the bath, she encouraged Kate to eat while soaking.

"There is sleepwear on the bed, because I can see you deserve a lie-down. Ring the bell when you need me."

Kate devoured the food, thanking God and the Yorks! She lingered in the bath until, with eyes drooping, she had to crawl into bed. She slept soundly in the dark, cool room and the scented, comforting bed.

E.P. STASZ

Alan, Alice and Dory discussed York's new refugee rescue.

"She's seems well-to-do, from the backpack evidence," said Dory. "I feel she's scared. Maybe she flees an abusive relationship. She had a folder with three thousand dollars. The other things in the backpack were a camera, "hooker" clothes and different makeup, varied-colored sunglasses and four different wigs."

Alice said, "I think the York brothers will have it disclosed soon and let us know. Dory, Kate's athletic looking but actually seems anemic."

Alan interrupted, "Let's wait for the info from the Yorks."

"Alice, maybe she travelled and didn't eat properly," Dory mused. "Remember, when stressed, people can lose their appetite. I'm going to have a walk, then sit with our gal." said Dory. The three York employees dispersed.

In her room Alice, set the alarm to prepare dinner, then flipped through her canvases and selected one that needed further work. She set it on the easel and compared various color chips for her next paint choice. It was a peaceful, useful, and fulfilling hobby for her. She dabbed paints on a palette and, thinking of their visitor, started to fix more colors on the canvas.

In Kate's room, Dory observes and hears Kate mumbling, moaning and thrashing with the blankets, but she still continues to sleep. Dory began softly singing her homeland songs—"My Wild Irish Rose," "Danny Boy," "Peggy O'Neil. She finished with "The Happy Wanderer," then and repeated the whole series.

Chapter 9

KATE WOKE, WONDERING WHERE SHE WAS. DARK. LUXURIANT bedding. It felt like home but she knew she had fled! She pinched herself to see she was dreaming. Nope!

"Kate, are you awake? It's Dory asking, dear one."

"I need some light. Where am I? What time is it? What day?"

Leaving the door open, Dory sat on the bed and captured Kate's hand. Patting it, she said, "It's safe here! It's safe here! I was right! You needed rest. This is the Yorks' home. Sam and Bob befriended you. They own a newspaper. The time is seven forty-five in the evening. It is June 26. When you're ready to get up, jeans and a T-shirt are at the end of the bed. Join us for the evening meal." Dory patted Kate's hand reassuringly. "You'll like it here. We are all like family. I worked as a nurse and a detective's assistant before I found this wonderful home to be a housekeeper. It's rewarding to work for the Yorks." The chatty housekeeper rose to go. "Kate, I see your aura needs changing to light and happiness. We will assist in redeeming it. See you soon."

Kate showered, dressed and started downstairs, noting the butler, Alan, waiting at the foot of the staircase. She asked to borrow a jacket, intending to walk the yard. He smiled. "I will walk with you. This jacket is right for the weather. I'll help you into it."

She nodded her thanks. The air was refreshing as they slowly walked the weaving trails through flowers and trees. She automatically put names to the plants as they walked. Squirrels and a variety of birds were abundant. They saw rabbits in the distance. There were horses enclosed in a corral, eagerly crunching a meal.

"Who owns the stables in the distance?" Kate asked.

"That's York land. There are horses, poultry, guard dogs and cats. They also have vegetable gardens and apple trees. We have strawberries, raspberries and gooseberries. All of it is overseen by a crew. It is outside the city boundary."

As they returned to the foyer, Sam was coming from his office.

"There you are, Kate! We've already dined on Alice's fabulous cooking. She's eager to meet you in the kitchen. Later we can eat dessert with drinks and meet a friend."

Alice Taylor warmly hugged Kate. "Welcome to my domain, Kate!

Kate ate while chatting with Alice, whose lovely personality brought comfort to Kate. A trim woman, standing only five feet in height, Alice happily displayed her yellow T-shirt and green jean overalls decked with food-related designs of fruit bowls, measuring spoons and coffee being poured into cups.

"We will have you cheery in no time. Eat! Eat!"

Kate ate, looking around and noting the restaurant-style six-burner gas range, the long wall of big windows revealing the gardens and the sleek black and gold concrete counters. She wondered where the refrigerator was. Alice opened it to retrieve a jug of fruit juice. It was disguised by the same material as the lower cabinets, just like in her own home. The kitchen was wonderfully scented by bowls of fresh flowers. It was cheerful and revealed the lingering glow of the day's twilight, seen through the big window over the sink. Kate relaxed and enjoyed the sage-stuffed pork chops, applesauce, rice with beans, and sliced tomatoes and cucumbers.

Alice said, "My mind is inquisitive. I worked in youth camps, at nursing and as a researcher for a newspaper and a legal office. Kate, visit me often in my gorgeous kitchen or the herb plot just outside."

Kate walked with Alice and Alan, carrying trays of beverages and dessert to Sam's office.

Alice and Alan left. Sam bounced up, eyes gleaming. "We've been discussing the odds of meeting on the tour bus. All here are committed to help you in the best possible way. Kate, meet Matt Neil, an FBI agent and a good friend."

Matt was dressed to relax—that was his best disguise. He stood six foot six, with a football linebacker's build and a head of curly blondish brown shaggy hair. A crinkly smile revealed blazing white teeth. His round face held glistening chocolate eyes.

The stranger stood and offered a hand to Kate. "I'm pleased to meet you. The FBI has been scrambling to locate you."

"Mr. Neil, show me ID please, like passport and driver's license." She copied both to her cell.

"Why the copying?" Matt inquired.

"Why not?" Kate retorted. "Why are the FBI searching for me? I have already been interviewed by one."

Matt turned to Kate. "Todd was working with the FBI. Who interviewed you?"

"Our FBI friend, Scott Hayes in New York."

"How did you travel? No one spotted you."

With big eyes she took a deep breath and replied, "I used cash, various transportation. I used an alias name. I just kept moving. Media attention would have devastated me. And the FBI never saved Todd – so how were they to protect me?"

"That was clever. No credit cards used! But I have some disturbing news. Agent Scott Hayes has been missing since June twenty-seventh."

"Why did he disappear? Scott informed me of the kidnapping. He had security cameras installed around my home. Had he been followed?"

Matt wanted to slow down the panic that was escalating. Closely watching Kate, he continued, "The FBI wanted to give you protection. They arranged for an identity change. I have a new passport for you to be Halley Coleman. The first name initial is often traced so they used a forceful one, Halley Comet, balanced with the light from Coleman. We can also change your fingerprints. Kate, it's now known that the Mob is responsible for the plane hit, so an identity change would be wise."

Kate loudly blew out a breath. "No other identity change! Just a new name. I'm a private person. I already wear disguises to deliver my art to the seller."

"Kate, just the fingerprints, no facial changes. Could you agree to that?"

"No. No. A new name alone means all kinds of papework, bank changes, driver's license, insurance, social security… That's enough! Scott's an ell and will work 24/7 to contact someone. He knew what I was doing. I didn't contact friends or family, so they would be safe. I called a security company to keep watch on our house. I reported to the chief of police,

Bryan, that I was leaving the state. I had to get away from the city, the Mob, Todd's employers, everyone. I needed to think. But this time without Todd is draining me. I'm really tired. Could I go to sleep again?"

Bob brought fresh tea for her and encouraged her to breathe deeply, sip and just focus on breathing. Soon her chin had fallen and she was nodding. Alan picked her up and carried her upstairs.

Dory was right behind and said, "I can shop for a new wardrobe for Kate. The clothes in the backpack are too large for her. I believe she's been travelling a lot. Did you notice how she directed Matt? That's a sign of authority, maybe she had servants."

Chapter 10

IN SEATTLE, BETH AND NICK WERE HAVING LUNCH WITH THE Yorks at Brandy's Home Flavors Restaurant. Knowing they were coming, the Yorks had a baby gift for Beth. She was delighted with the baby cutlery engraved with the family name and the smart set of rompers for a toddler.

Beth talked non-stop about her plans for the family and how they would raise their child. Nick and the Yorks winked at each other as she rambled, barely eating.

"You're very careful with your diet?" Bob asked, with eyebrows raised at Beth.

"My Phil is the diet watcher, making me the same. Must protect the baby, you know."

Finishing his flan, leaning back Nick said, " I really—"

"Hello, friends!" Smile beaming, Beth's friend Mavis had come behind Nick and leaned over to kiss him. She moved on to the Yorks, who raised her hands and kissed her knuckles.

"Is the meal finished? Good! I'm taking Beth with me. We've shopping to do, Beth, and so little time to do it!" laughed Mavis.

*   *   *

Late that afternoon, in the newspaper office, Nick Farrell shook his head at Sam and Bob.

"An amazing bus ride, again. How do you two draw out and rescue the victims? It's like breathing with you!" He grinned and got down to business. "How can my service be used? Just like the paper business, you've plotted my action."

"Your background in detective research is the key," said Sam. "We have 'Halley' resting now but we need to get her moving. She's an active personality, and we can't keep her cooped up here or she will burst from inactivity. Use her on some trails. We mentioned the Red Rock to her while we had supper, and she looked enthused about working in the outdoors."

"Jan in Tacoma is now only open 7a.m. to 10 p.m. She also needs help and we could stash Halley there," said Nick. "Jan is very tired, Bob, so we better find her some relief."

"I'll see to it," replied Bob.

"Has anyone had word yet from Scott or Bruce? I'm on vacation currently and will do some detecting. But I'm wondering how easily I can fit in? It's possible Halley may overload with having to deal with another new face. How did she address you and Matt?"

Sam laughed. "Show your driver's license and passport when you meet! Have all the family at once to meet her. See if she would do the driving, saying your testing her strengths. Talk about your hiking trails. Stay the night. The usual room is ready for you, and you can use my office computer. Avoid e-mails that use her name, old or new. Stress is her enemy. I hope something shakes soon." Sam stifled a yawn. "I'm heading to bed. Call Alan if you need anything else."

Chapter 11

SCOTT HAYES CLICKED ONTO SADIE ON HIS PHONE, WHICH after several minutes connected with Kate's cell. Alice answered and gave Scott the third degree to learn about him.

"That confirms what I learned about the Scott we discussed this afternoon. Give me your message, and it will go to the person needing it," Alice said.

Scott in turn, wanted Alice to identify her status. When he was satisfied, he said, "Okay, Alice. Let the Yorks' friend, Agent Neil, know I'm a mole in the NY Mob. I uncovered…"

At five a.m., Alice gave the message to Alan.

"I knew Agent Scott was working with the Denvers," he confirmed. "I'll contact Matt on all this."

Alan came from a wealthy background. His father, an attorney, had Alan trained in martial arts and researching cases for him. Alan had served with the London Ambulance and worked in private investigations. He had further experience working several assignments with Matt. His voracious appetite for learning had led him to become skilled in management and public relations, making him very valuable to the Yorks. At the local pub he sang and joked with the locals and tourists. He was a master at disguises and careful to change his voice and comments from the usual.

Halley, he thought, was about to have her luck changed now that she was in the Yorks' sphere. Thanks too to Matt for setting up the needed permanent changes from Kate to Halley. Seeing she was close to exhaustion when the Yorks met her, the arrangements were immediately organized. She needed rest and what better way to recover. Healing would come with love showered on her. This group was good at that.

Chapter 12

AT THE YORKS' HOME, NICK HAD FALLEN ASLEEP AT THE COMputer. He awoke hearing someone calling.

"Sam. Sam. No one in… in… hep… meee." There was a thud, and Nick quickly turned on a light and approached the bundled form on the floor. It must be Halley. He took her pulse, noting the slow beat. At his elbow Alan appeared.

"Nick, I'll take her back to bed. You bring the tea from the kitchen."

In the bedroom, Alan supported Halley's head as she sipped her sleep aid. He checked her eyes, then tucked the comforter under her chin and hips.

As the men returned to the office, Nick rasked, "Do you think she was abused?"

Alan shook his head. "No. I think she was running scared. We also need sleep before morning."

"So right, Alan. So right."

Alan and Dory cared for Halley. They kept her in sleep mode to heal her exhaustion. They gave her protein drinks, more liquids and regular doses of the drugs that sent her back to sleep. Dory moves her limbs as she sleeps.

Surfacing from sleep, Halley battled the dizziness and blackness and struggled to sit. She moaned, "I'm in prison. Todd…. Todd. Come back. Come. Come." She continued to mumble in her drugged sleep, "Wrecking… wrecking… no home… not safe… why… call… call… run… pack… run…"

Another time, her thoughts groggy, she walked with Todd on the beach, laughing and tossing rocks to ripple the water. Groaning in her sleep, she said, "Serenity… serenity… oh, merciful God." Head bursting, she struggles to wake up. She must stay alert. She must run to safety. Where? Where? She tosses and turns, making the sheets wrap tightly around her. Her mind sinks into black oblivion.

*   *   *

Alan, Alice and Dory were in the tropics room, discussing how to deal with helping Halley to recover and get on with living after such personal tragedy and her long flight.

"My research revealed that Halley is a photographer and painter. Look at these." Alan showed them photos he obtained from Belle's Gallery in New York City.

Dory and Alice exclaim, "Wow… wow!"

Alice continues, "Marvellous colors. They make me feel really alive, there's so much movement in them! Hey, are they signed, Alan?"

"Sure, Alice. But she used an alias name, to keep her life private. Didn't you notice her understated wedding rings?"

Dory asked, "Could we talk freely with Kate—sorry, Halley—about her work?"

"No! Let's work subtly. I'll find out what cameras she used. Maybe placing them on view in her bedroom will encourage

E.P. STASZ

Halley to talk. And Alice, you paint, discuss it with her. Do you have some work and supplies here?"

"I'm not a hotshot painter like her!"

"We all do what we can, some do better than others. Show that you 'dabble' in painting then. I for one would like to see your work!"

"Alan, Halley had a camera in her backpack," said Dory. "I'll bring it and you buy some film. This gal loves that Halley. She's gifted, generous, helpful, and deeply loves her man!"

Alice shyly invited Alan to view her work and they left.

Chapter 13

HOT DISCUSSION WAS FLOWING AMONG THE LEGAL PARTNERS Lloyd Hardy, Ben Hanson and Jack Kendel. Lawyers being long-winded, they had been talking for over an hour. Hanson finally remarked, "We never had Todd aboard with us on the Mob business. Less to share with. Hah, hah. I enjoy the firm's work on wills and estates."

The intercom buzzed and suddenly the door opened to reveal what appeared to be a rattily dressed homeless guy. He looked around, then shuffled over to Lloyd Hardy and handed him a package. Hardy reached into his briefcase and removed another package, giving it to the "homeless" man, who shuffled out the door.

Jack Kendel was the most ambitious of the partners. He had approached Hardy to become a partner in the firm, and that had panned out. Kendel played tennis and basketball with Todd and other community fellows. He also had a genius mind with computers and had discovered some of the mob's dealings. He had worked with mercenaries. Jack turned to his appointed Chief and asked, "Lloyd, can you clarify if Todd was a Mob mole?"

Lloyd replied, "Todd was doing his job here and bringing in more clients, which benefitted us, so why suspect him of ingenuity? Jack, you had him move in with us to help with the court cases. It worked! Get your ducks in a row. We have two hundred clients and there is work to finish. I'll take over Todd's."

Jack would not be put off. "Who tried to wreck the plane? That slick Mobguy, Mel Steffes, was hustling Todd to date his daughter Lynn. I know they did meet a few times. She's a real looker and has intelligence. Lately, Steffes has been sending his guys—Scott or Bruce—with the bundles. Steffes said he was training them since Boss Loren was soon to retire and Steffes was next in command. He often commented, 'You can't trust delivery guys too long, soon their positions must change to avoid boredom and sloppiness. The mob's always on alert for discrepancies.' Mel wants to bring in some females to deliver. These changes will be happening and we may no longer be even used. Consider what I've reported."

"Why do the deliveries come in office hours?" asked Ben "Have the secretaries clued to the happenings?"

Ben Hanson said, "We don't discuss with the help what we do on the side, do we?"

Hardy countered, "Only the three of us are in the deal. We keep it restricted! I never ordered a hit. But we know the Mob regularly orders hits. Would they target a plane? I don't know. All we can do now is keep our ears and eyes alert. Return to your office work."

Hardy sat in his office and considered Jack's information. With Jack's background, the FBI would be on his case shortly. He considered how he could protect his own interests and keep Jack from the FBI's clutches. Last week Steffes had asked if Jack was an FBI mole. Hardy didn't think so.

Steffes and his father, Boss Loren, did investments and taxes with Jack, who often consulted with Hardy about it. Hardy had some worry about the work covered. Steffes also wanted Hardy to determine if there was a mole trying to undermine the mob. This was modern times. Steffes had confided that he really didn't want the Mob business; however leaving the business would be terminating his life. Lynn hated it all and wanted to disappear.

Hardy considered: *I'm sixty, a widower, no children, and lately seriously giving thought to retiring.* The easy Mob money made him rich and he was losing interest in legal work. *What would I do, if I retired? Who had tried to blow up the plane? Why wait for FBI contact—should I contact them?* Many questions and no answers.

Lloyd stored his overlooked correspondence, locked the drawers and cabinets. Picking up his briefcase, locked his office and left. He was still musing as he walked to his car and after tossing his briefcase on the back seat, he turns and was confronted by Mob Boss Loren Steppes himself and two minions.

"We want you at a meeting with our rival, Steve Giovanni. Meet us at the Dock restaurant tonight at ten." The Mob boss turned, protected front and back by the minions, and walked away before Hardy could speak.

Hardy was shocked at the request, even more so because the Boss came in person to relate the demand. Could the meeting concern Mel Steffes? Hardy determined to get in touch with the younger Steffes and learn more.

Chapter 14

NICK FARRELL HAD RESEARCHED WEATHER AND LOCAL events in the week before and the day of the attempt to bomb the airplane. What had been in the shipping lanes? He also contacted his family at Red Rock, informing them what the Yorks had proposed.

Where, he wondered, were Halley's workstations for photography and painting?

He left for the kitchen, hoping for breakfast and a chat with Alice—but Alice asked him to speak with Sam or Alan for updates.

* * *

Dory looked in on Halley, hoping she'd be able to start recuperating in the outdoors. Adjacent to Halley's room, Dory set the shower running with the drain stopped so the tub would fill, then added bubble bath for fun. "Come Halley, sit on the bench and enjoy the refreshing water. Ring this bell when you're ready for your hair wash, okay?"

"Mmm–hum… mm-hum."

Half an hour later, feeling alive and so much better, Halley dressed in the delicate rose-colored undies and purple sweat-suit laid on the bed. Dory came in to help and revealed her hairdressing skill on Halley's mahogany mane.

"It's shorter than I remember," remarked Halley. "Oh, I lost weight !"

"Halley, you were exhausted, so don't fret! You're a beautiful woman. It takes time to adjust, however you have done well this past week. Alice has brunch for us in the tropical observatory. Ready for taking the walk?"

"Okay."

At the top of the stairs, Halley slipped her arm around Dory's waist. "I need confidence."

"I have been there, sweetheart. I'll support you and so will everyone else in this house!"

* * *

Ghost, the Yorks' sleek, whitewashed cat, sat high up on a beam in the observatory, scrutinizing the people below through sparkling green eyes. Soon Ghost was stretching a leg up and grooming himself.

"Halley, eat more food and tea," urged Dory. They sat surrounded by tropical plants and butterflies.

Halley stammered, "I'm still wobbly... body and head. Juice, tea... that's all I need... for awhile. This place is very pleasing... to the senses. I could... rest here."

"Just stretch out on the lounge. Ghost will likely curl up with you. I'll let you relax as I check in with Alice," replied Dory.

Startled, Halley asked "Ghost? What ghost?"

E.P. STASZ

"Sorry. I thought you'd met our resident Ghost. See up there?" She pointed to the beam. "That is Ghost!"

"Beautiful, just like the butterflies." Halley sipped her juice and leaned back on the lounge. Soon she was asleep. Ghost walked over to her, sniffing, then circled and lay by her feet.

Nick entered the observatory carrying his coffee. He was strolling the aisles when he noticed someone asleep on the lounge. As he moved near, there was Ghost curled asleep by her feet. Viewing the lunch food under glass, he selected a scone and strawberries to munch and studied the beauty sleeping. This must be Halley!

He slowly walked the observatory, observing all the changes since he last visited. On his way out, he noted that Ghost was now sleeping on Halley's chest.

Two hours later, Dory returned. "Halley, time to rise. We can walk around to ease your muscles and then you can sleep again."

Halley stretched and groaned. "Okay." Ghost rose and sauntered away. "Yes. Good. I must get moving." She looked puzzled. "My chest is very warm."

"Have some water or juice first."

They slowly meandered through the lush plants, Halley breathing deeply, like a runner. Dory focused her attention on beauties hidden within the foliage.

Returning to the brunch area, they found fresh tea, finger sandwiches, stuffed mushrooms and macaroons. Halley was able to eat now, and they snacked together. Halley looked very tired to Dory.

"You'd best rest now; I'll be back later to check on you."

Smiling, sagging into the lounge cushions, Halley said, "Okay. I could use another sleep."

"Alan, Alan," called Dory as she walked into the study. Not there. She went to search the kitchen but before reaching it, ran into Alice.

"Dory, Alan is with Sam and Nick in the den. Can I help you?"

"Do you think, Alice, the sleep aid was too potent for Halley? She is still groggy and weak. I need confirming. It's a new drug to me."

"Halley was not nauseated, so that is the most significant. I think we need to know how much she travelled before meeting the Yorks. She was very tired when she arrived here, and you stated her clothes were too big. Maybe she is anemic. Ask the Yorks to contact the doctor. He or she should have run blood checks."

"When I meditated, I saw her working at a feverish pace, painting and the room had many more paintings leaning against a long aisle support," said Dory. "There was a door labelled RED… Stay OUT! She and Todd are deeply in love. In her early life she was surrounded with loving people, perhaps her family. Let Alan and Sam know. I'll return and watch over her. Alice, can we have more tea and goodies in two hours, when I wake her?"

When the time came, Dory began to sing rather loudly as she sat by Halley, who stirred, and sighed. Dory started dancing lightly on the patio flooring and continued to sing her Irish pub tunes. Turning to gaze at Halley, she halted, as Halley was softly laughing, looking at her.

"Oh! To be so free and easy with life! Teach me, teach me!"

"Up with you, young Miss! A quick refreshing shower and we will begin enjoying life. Come! Place some spring in your step for the upcoming festivities."

"Yes, Nurse. I'll take all your help." She slipped her hand around Dory's waist, and they shuffle-danced out of the observatory.

Chapter 15

AT THE DOCK RESTAURANT, RIVAL MOB BOSSES LOREN STEFFES and Steve Giovanni and the lawyer, Lloyd Hardy, were greeted by the owner, Patrick Stone. He led them to the special private table for their business discussion.

Giovanni was a stocky five foot three, beaming with smiles. He wore a sharply tailored navy pinstripe suit, a deep blue shirt, and a white tie with designs in deep blue. His thick fingers were bejewelled with rings.

Steffes was six feet tall, with a lean frame with short and silvery curly hair. He wore a midnight black tailored suit with a grey patterned silk shirt and a vest of silvery black. His hands only displayed a garnet ring on the left, and on the right a large onyx. He cautiously eyed the surroundings, then pumped the hand of his rival.

The two men enthused over the platter of Italian appetizer delicacies. They munched with gusto, drinking wine and discussing family, football, movies and operas.

The servers stood, polished and spine stiffened, ready to fill more drink orders. Other servers anxiously waited to serve the main meal.

Giovanni boosted, "Orders are on me. Eat up. Eat up."

They ate heartily. Servers were dismissed as the two men turned to business.

Giovanni stated, "All of my members were saved from the attempted plane disaster. Lloyd, have you learned who was responsible?"

"Even the FBI have no proof," replied Hardy. "They suspect terrorists. An unidentified person was captured on airport video, working inside with the luggage loading. They are following up."

Giovanni puffed on his cigar and remarked, "Our people will learn sooner than the FBI. Tonight we concentrate on the changes we want. Lloyd can be the mediator for today's business. Face it, Loren, we are not getting younger ourselves. I had six relatives come to me two months ago, and now several new families will come. They are young and ambitious. We'll be making changes. I hope you stay to your area and I will stay to mine."

"Changes! What other changes? Are you intending to employ women in the work, or setting women in soliciting positions?" asked Steffes.

"What talk is this?"

"Is the traditional business being expanded?"

"Accountants always needed too many books. By using computers, our work has simplified. When the new people arrive, other things will be discussed."

"I heard that the FBI and police have moles in our business," said Steffes. "I have checked ours."

"I suspected that months ago and took precautions earlier. We check regularly," Giovanni assured him. "Your granddaughter, Lynn, is not yet married? Could there be a meet-up with my young men?"

"She is very independent! I do not force issues on her."

"Meeting for introductions, only dear friend. We can show that here, this country, is more friendly, not so vicious. Cooperation with the other forces works best."

"We should meet again after your new arrivals have settled in."

"Good!"

They firmly clasped hands and exited the Dock, flanked by their respective muscle men.

Lloyd, who was dismissed without being acknowledged, muttered to himself, "Guess that's why they are the Mob." He was buttoning his overcoat when a sudden loud blast outside shook the building. As he turned to the window, another loud blast was heard, and he and other startled patrons saw flames across and up the street.

The restaurant buzzed with shocked conversations.

"Where were we parked?"

"Call 911!"

"Was it a crash?"

"Oh, no! People must be hurt! Call for the ambulance!"

Other people hurried onto the sidewalk and street to check the happenings. Sirens wailed! Fire trucks rushed in and began pumping chemicals over the explosion area. Ambulances arrived, ready for the worst. Police rushed the area.

At the Dock, three policemen entered to canvas information from clients, hoping to find eyewitnesses. They quickly work through the diners, tape-recording their accounts, and asking them to call if they find their car is missing.

Then they question the Dock owner, Patrick Stone.

E.P. STASZ

"Just before the loud explosion, who had left the restaurant?"

"I never noticed. We had a heavy crowd as usual."

"Did you or the servers notice any table arguments?"

Stone shook his head. "It was calm, except for laughter and enjoyment."

"Earlier today, were there any unusual occurences here?"

"No. We are a respectable establishment!"

"Keep the restaurant closed until we notify you otherwise."

Lloyd knew about accidents and police. He had quickly left through the back kitchen door before their arrival to avoid being questioned. He had enough problems without adding this. He wondered who was hurt. Could it be a rival gang war?

Patrick Stone telephoned Mel Steffe and explained the happenings. He assured Steffe there was no connection made to his name. It was unknown what and who were the target.

Steffe asked Stone to get a canvas bag and retrieve the items attached below the bosses' table, once everyone had left. They arranged to meet four blocks south to exchange the bag. He cautioned Stone to stay calm.

The younger Steffe had, prior to the evening, enlisted Stone's help. Steffe had placed disguised recording devices beneath the table, to keep himself informed.

By the next day, the media was rampantly reporting news of the blast and offering a reward to anyone who had conclusive information on the night's event.

* * *

Two men were in a beach house two hours from the Dock, watching the television news. They had already read the papers. They eyed each other and clapped high fives. Using vinyl gloves and cleaners, they wiped down all surfaces and door knobs and carried the garbage bags to their rental vehicle. Before they drive away, they pull on fine leather gloves. A mile away they stop and place the garbage bags in a large restaurant trash bin.

Leaving the rental in Trenton, they grabbed a bus heading to Washington, DC. For two day they traveled on tour buses, always tracking the news. They flew to Montreal, Canada and toured that city. They were well versed in several languages, but French was their mother tongue. On the sixth day at six o'clock, they checked their new bank accounts for new deposits. It was there! They wired their money through several stops, then flew back to their home abroad.

Chapter 16

IN THE EVENING, A REFRESHED HALLEY ENTERED THE DINING room. She was met by Sam and Bob York and a stranger. Bob introduced her to Nick, from Red Rock Resort.

"Good to meet you, Nick. Sam and Bob told me your resort holds classes and offers guided hiking. I like hiking."

Nick offered a friendly smile. "Besides hiking, the classes are for increasing an individual's well-being. How much do you hike?"

"I had a routine of running daily and hiked twice a month."

Sam and Bob nodded to each other. It looked like the patient was recovering.

They dined on broiled pepper steak, twice-baked potatoes with parsley butter, creamed kale and a side salad of greens, beets, carrots and cucumbers. Discussion turned to the previous night's news of blasted cars at the NYC Dock restaurant.

Sam noticed that Halley was toying with her food, only taking tiny amounts. "How are you feeling now, Halley?" he asked. "Not too hungry, yet?" He smiled with a lifted eyebrow.

Halley shone glistening eyes at Sam. "I've laid around too much. I need action to really achieve good health and appetite.

News of that blast brings memories. I'm thankful for the help from York and associates, but I've never sat much before. I want to start some things. I feel refreshed."

Alan stood suddenly and invited them to go to the library for dessert and coffee.

In the library, Alice and Alan distributed drinks and plates of mixed fresh fruit and clotted cream, with a bite of fudge as garnish. Alice winked at Halley, pointing to her three pieces of fudge.

Alan informed them that Matt left a message. "Halley's home has been put under a company name and Halley's girl-friends are living in it."

Sam placed an arm around her shoulder and said, "Does this info on your home relieve some stress?"

"Yes. Yes. I was so scared, I did not think of all the angles to stay undercover!"

Sam beckoned Nick over. "Halley, Nick's family has invited you to stay with them out at the resort. The outdoors will do you good!"

Nick adds, "Would you like to come with me tomorrow and we'll tour the place? Mom and Dad, my sister Beth and her husband Phil are anxious to meet you. At dinner you mentioned the need for action, and we can supply that by hiring you to guide or whatever."

"Yes, Nick, thank-you. I need to move and get myself in shape. You won me over to your side when you mentioned a job outdoors! That is exceptional for me! I'll be able to really breathe!" She hesitated. "First, though... can you show me your driver's license, Nick?"

Nick complied and Halley placed it on her phone.

Nick grinned. "Let's meet and go after breakfast."

E.P. STASZ

"I hope to rise early tomorrow. Lucky for us, Alice likes an early start."

"Do you have any hobbies, Halley?" Nick was careful to keep the question casual.

"Oh. I dabble with paints and camera. I also like gardening."

"You will love shooting and painting our area of Red Rock."

Dory entered the library. "Hello, Nick! Have you been too busy to visit much this summer? We miss you. Just look at you! All tanned like a movie star!"

"Hello, lovely Dory, let's make a date to to watch some movies and have dinner—or better yet, join us for early breakfast tomorrow!" Smiling, he wrapped her in a bear hug.

"You are such a rascal!" She cuffed his arm playfully. "I have my beauty sleep to catch up on. I'll leave with Halley so she'll be well rested by morning. Come, sweet lady."

Alan came in and said to Sam, "You are one smooth operator. Halley never questioned your help. She even said, 'Lucky me, the Yorks saw through me!'"

"Well, that's really good! We've got help for Halley, help for Jan and now it's over to Nick. We only need to monitor now. Stay on it, Alan. The FBI sure is slow to determine Todd's whereabouts."

Chapter 17

DRESSED IN LIGHTWEIGHT JEANS AND RED T-SHIRT COVERED with a blue light jacket, Halley entered the kitchen and hugged Alice. She took in the cook's purple pantsuit, covered with a black apron printed with bright sunflowers, and hugged her again, saying, "Here's another for your wonderful get up!"

"Thanks. My, my, look at you! Rosy cheeks, a fancy braid, and is there a big appetite with them?"

"Yes, Mom! I ran with the horses. It was exhilarating! I did my daily three miles. Let me hug you twice." Alice beams, thanking Halley for the loving term "Mom."

"Alice you outdid yourself again! Waffles, strawberry sauce, whipped cream, scrambled eggs, salmon, mixed juices." Halley admired the bountiful spread. "It's wonderfully presented." They loaded their plates and sat to enjoy.

"Halley," Alice asked carefully, "Have you expressed your feelings on the loss of Todd?"

"He needs healing. He will return! I had the habit of Prayer before I met Todd. He was quick to endorse the practice. I showed him Mother Teresa's words: 'Prayer makes your heart bigger, until it is capable of containing the gift of God himself.'"

Halley decided to open her heart to her new friend. "Todd showered me in wildflowers he picked and even selected those he wanted for unique arrangements made at the florist's. We tracked the night sky through the seasons, noting the changing positions of the constellations—evidence of God's marvellous works! Ursa Major, that's the Big Dipper. It is part of the Great Bear stars and you follow upward to find the North Star beyond. It's important to know the North Star location to find your way if you're lost in a forest or on hiking trails. I grew up in the northern province and we learned the importance of star recognition early.

"We loved dancing! We shared our deepest feelings! We could discuss anything. We had even discussed death. I don't feel he is gone!" She shook her head, and repeated, "I still don't feel he is really gone, gone. Yet, my life was invaded and I left. All that attention from the police, FBI, and media would have devastated me. I wanted to be invisible. I had used disguises to stay private and anonymous with my work. My family is close, but they see me as different because I think and act outside the box.

"Dory says, here you are all like family. That is the vibration I felt in this house, which comforted me." Pausing for breath, she looked into Alice's eyes. "Do you and Dory have psychic senses? What I mean…"

"Coffee! Coffee!" The doors were flung open and Alan and Nick entered.

"Good thing I have swinging doors, fellows. Please serve yourself."

Alice turned toward Halley and continued, "I like my sunshine and warmth, none of the snow, slush, getting dressed in layers nor getting my car stuck. You adapted to the rigours of the weather up north. Do you miss it now, Halley?"

Halley giggled. "It gives one appreciation of season changes and God's wonderful creations, Alice. What I avoid are mountains that rob the sun before the day is gone, but that's in British Columbia. When driving for business is essential, I dislike ice, snowy conditions, or very heavy rain. Otherwise it's just daily living."

"Halley, I've had two coffees and can now carry on a conversation." Alan grinned at her. "Alice, you pamper us with the wonderful food. Thanks!"

"I second the motion and perhaps Alice can pack us a lunch, right Halley?" Nick teased, winking at Alice. Facing the beauty again he asked "Have you hiking gear? "

"Hat, boots, jeans and layers of sweaters, survival kit, water bottles, backpack. What else is needed?"

"Extra socks, rain gear, swimsuit and when at the resort, casual wear, dance heels and dress," Nick quickly replied.

"I'll soon get to it, Nick. Alan and Alice, who placed film in my room?"

"Scott had informed us of your work. The family thought bringing back a piece of your past would comfort and help you to move forward," said Alan.

"I already stowed it in my bag, hoping they were for me to use! Thank you, all."

Sam and Bob entered and called, "Good morning, everyone."

Bob continued, "I'm glad we arrived to see you off, Halley. The resort is a great place. When Sam and I became widowers, Mike and Trudy scooped us up and made us join the living again! Halley, we will continue to keep in touch with you. We consider you our daughter!"

Halley raised her head and arms, saying, "Concourse on High, bless my new guardians!' She wiped her tears.

"It's okay, Halley. You have love from all of us," emphasized Bob.

Halley hugged Bob tightly and went to Sam to do the same. Eyes holding back more tears, she quietly said, "I accept the wisdom of your years. Now that I know this family, you won't ever be rid of me." She hugged Alice and Alan and left to finish packing.

"Nick, take good care of our adopted daughter!"

Chapter 18

ARRIVING AT THE RED ROCK RESORT OVERLOOK, NICK gently shook Halley's shoulder.

"Hmm.... what?" She slowly woke to bright sunshine and a hand on her shoulder. She looked across at Nick, and widening her eyes said, "I thought I was in bed dreaming."

Laughing, Nick confirmed, "You may have been dreaming. You were asleep within five minutes of leaving the Yorks'. But we'll soon have you moving and getting balanced in health. Look!" He pointed to the scene in front of them. "This is Red Rock Resort."

He had parked on a high cliff for an overview photo shoot. The lookout revealed the grand resort and surrounding vistas and vivid sparkling waters. Halley saw people windsurfing, riding the currents.

"It is a beautiful vision, Nick. Let me snap this scene."

Later, as Nick drove toward the resort, he explained that they employed sixty people as hostesses, cooks, and guides, and in housekeeping, the gift shop and ground maintenance. "Plus we staff classes in Ti Chi, Yoga, Meditation, Bereavement

Counselling, Fire Pit Poetry, and Security," In the heavy traffic of summer and fall, he explained, they beefed up the security.

"I'll hike a lot until I feel comfortable around all the guests," said Halley.

"We keep the family living quarters separate from the public."

"I'll ease into some public encounters!" she exclaimed.

"Go at your own pace, Halley. Meet my family, that's only four people." He took her hand in his, leading her up the steps, into the family's part. She was jolted by his cold hand.

Put that aside for now, she thought. Concentrate on hope and the plan for her recovery.

Nick led her to the hot tub, stating, "This is where I unwind after hiking." Then he showed her the conservatory of lush green plants, displaying splendid colors. There were two resident parrots and water cascading down a wall. The place was filled with varieties of orchids.

Beyond this room, they wound around a twisty trail onto more steps and into a foyer of black and white tiles. To their left was a kitchen, opening to a vaulted ceiling over a dining area and a large sitting room. Windows lined one wall, revealing the splendour of the outdoors. The rooms were light green, with bright accents of blue, yellow and red in cushions, furniture, drapery and pictures.

Nick's parents entered from the public side, carrying big containers with kitchen labels. Beaming a big smile, Mike Farrell said, "Howdy," setting his container on the dinner table. He stretched out his arm and shook Halley's hand, searching her eyes. "I'm pleased to finally meet you, Halley. Sam and Bob claim you as daughter! Praise the Lord for bringing you to them!"

Trudy set her container beside Mike's. She turned, circling her arms around Halley. "May the Lord bless you, Halley, in strength, in courage, in trust and in His care." She hugged her again.

"Mom, we could use tea now!" Mike left to prepare it, leaving Trudy to sit and visit.

"Alan phoned and said you were on the way. We have snacks and Mike is already making tea. I'll wash up and be back in a jiff." Trudy moved swiftly to wash and bring back a tray of cups, lemon, cream and sugar.

Mike sat by Halley and offered his sympathy on her loss of Todd. He related that last year his brother and wife had lost a teenager, their nephew, to murder. It was on April 17 and their nephew had his birthday that day. "When the evil man was captured a month later, the police learned that our Gerry was his seventeenth victim. We pray God will forgive him. We are working on forgiveness too."

By then Nick had poured the tea and Trudy had set out fresh vegetables, strawberry and peach turnovers, cheesy muffins, and ham and cream cheese on toasted rye.

They talked about some of the happenings at the resort, especially the animals that had been spotted. A comedian had just left after several days entertaining the guests.

The enthused parents pointed out the window at the varied special spots. They shared that Beth and Phil were in Portland, Oregon and would be back in two days.

"Halley, let's go to your room. Your bags should be there now."

Halley joined Trudy and they walked into a hall and climbed the stairs, which had one side lined with various dream catchers. Halley slowed to examine them. "My, this is a wonderful display of Native art! How did you collect them?"

"Some of our clients and employees make them especially for us. They were presented as gifts, to reward us for the healing they found here. I understand they had ancient blessings placed on them. There is an amazing story for each person who made one."

They turned right at the top of the staircase and went past three doors before stopping at a door topped with a stained glass transom. As she opened the door, Trudy said, "This is yours for as long as you want to stay."

A large window, set off by two soft reading chairs and a small table holding an array of colored gems, looked out over a beautiful outdoor vista. Noting the warm beige and chocolate furnishings and piles of cheery pillows, Halley exclaimed, "This is an enchanting room, Trudy. Thank you."

"You have your own bathroom. Good, the bags are here. Will you rest or go out now?"

"I think Nick kept silent on our drive here so I could sleep. Now I'm ready to roam! I just need my hat, hiking boots and backpack."

*   *   *

Nick opened out a map of the area trails, commenting they would start on number one, since it was shortest, and Halley could have the rest of the afternoon off. The map showed it as a two-hour hike for excellent hikers. He showed her where all the trails were, the remarkable sites, and which animals were likely to be spotted. All this was marked on the map.

"Here's your personal map for your backpack. I keep mine in my pocket."

"Okay, let's go!" Halley was impatient. They started out and Halley stressed to Nick that she preferred quiet hiking.

She had the camera hanging around her shoulder and neck. After forty-five minutes, she was ready for a drink of water. There was a viewpoint just ahead. Gazing across the expansive valley, she spotted someone paragliding. Later she spied, a fox and her two kits. Halley snapped the fox. She laughed and laughed. She had, since the start of her flight from New York, continually stopped and offered healing prayers for Todd. She raised her arms and shouted, "O Thou Glory of the most Glorious!" She walked toward Nick, exclaiming, "It's remarkable! Our spirits soar when we witness God's wonders."

Later they crossed a rope bridge stretched over a river far below. As they rounded the cliff and headed into a meadow, there, sitting on a rock in the sun, were two weary men. Halley went pale and silently stood rooted to her spot. Nick greeted them. Only the men exchanged names.

One inquired, "How far to the next station? We left from Old Man House at nine this morning."

Nick asked, "How are you feeling? You look worn out."

The first man, Pete, said, "I'm weak. We ran out of water."

Frank slowly remarked, "I'm a bit dizzy. Weak too."

Nick led them to sit in the shade, then brought out his map and using the Ranger Tower, called for a medical helicopter. Response time would be fifteen minutes.

While waiting, the men said they had loving wives who had been killed when their car crashed. The men had been devastated and decided to take an extended leave from work for a new outlook.

Halley had been silent, wetting a cloth to wipe Frank's face and neck. She repeats the action for Pete. Both men have been given water to sip slowly.

"Do you work as a nurse or perform in Nashville?" Frank asked Halley.

She looked at Nick and signed with her hands, "I'm deaf mute."

"Sorry, Miss, my misstep, you look familiar."

The helicopter arrived, interrupting further conversation. Paramedics quickly checked Pete and Frank vitals and questioned them. Leaving more water with Halley and Nick, they left with the weakened men.

"Nick, I would like to return now. That scene was unnerving. I wasn't ready to encounter strangers."

They are silent returning to the resort. Halley scrambled into her room for a hot bath. Nick looked after informing the other resort guides and sent photos of the 'rescued' men to the Rangers.

Out of the bath, Halley went to sleep, awakening three hours later. She heard singing and turned her head to see Trudy doing Tai Chi exercises.

"Trudy! Have you been watching over me?" joked Halley.

"Dory phoned and asked me to. Come on love, have a shower!"

Chapter 19

HALLEY ENTERED THE KITCHEN AND FOUND SAM AND DORY there. "Halley, we came to see how you are doing," said Sam. Alice and Dory hugged her. When Sam hugged her, she whispered, "Take me home with you!"

In the Farrells' kitchen there was chicken soup, fresh biscuits, and trays of varied cheeses, veggies and fruits.

"Come into my dining parlour, said the spider to the fly! Is that how you feel, Halley?" Nick was grinning.

"I'm just hungry. I can't relate to anything but food right now, sorry."

They tucked into the food. Sam and Nick talked quietly.

"Halley, were the two men on the trail known to you?" Nick asked. She silently shook her head no.

Nick said, "I took photos of them on my phone and sent the pics to the Rangers, asking them to run a security check. The Rangers sent Pete and Frank's driver licenses to the FBI. Both licenses are employed by the Mob. The FBI will investigate the men to find out the real story of why they were using fake ID and using those names."

Sam, Dory, Alice and Halley leave to walk and think.

*　*　*

The FBI agent Matt Neil arrived, and Nick explained what had happened.

"Interesting." Matt sat silently thinking. "First, is there any coffee and dessert available?"

Nick prepared a tray of ham and cheese sandwiches, pickles, and fruit dessert for Matt.

Eating, Matt related, "Halley and Todd are good friends with Scott Hayes. We still don't have any information about Todd's whereabouts."

"I think, Matt we need to check with the moles and get their latest findings, and let them know what happened here," suggested Nick. "Fax them the hikers' photos and licences."

"I can do that, Nick. Good idea. See you soon."

*　*　*

The walkers returned at about eight o'clock and entered the living room.

"Halley, what did you sign to me when we were with the weary men?" asked Nick.

"Just that I was deaf mute, so I could stay unidentified. I was not ready for any confrontation."

Sam came over and hugged Halley. "This has been a busy, disjointed time for you."

"Oh, why haven't the FBI found Todd yet?" said Halley, teary-eyed. Dory hugged her.

"Wait, Dory! Eyes reveal the soul so maybe he is fey and reads auras?"

" No. No, Halley. The fey must harm no one."

Dory and Halley returned to the bedroom. Alice spoke briefly with Sam, then quickly joined the two women. She looked to Halley and said, "You're a noted painter and photographer. Come back with us tonight. I'll show you my efforts at painting."

"Good, Alice. I'll go thank Trudy and Mike."

Chapter 20

BACK IN SEATTLE, THE LADIES QUICKLY MOVED TO ALICE'S bedroom, where she had hung two of her paintings. Halley looked at Dory, then Alice, with questioning eyes.

"What's this little painting? Look closely at this hilly field of sunflowers, the curvy road, the faded colors in the pickup pulling a horse trailer, that marvellous variegated barn and windmill, the forest and in the far distance the misty hills. All is set dark against light, giving marvellous perspective and sharpness in the color contrasts. The movement catches the beholder's eye—the dust behind the pickup, the motion on the weather vane, the twisting branches and foliage and the feathering in the clouds. It's all beautiful and deeply felt. Where did you study—or is this an inherited inner strength?"

"I've travelled different countries and spent time in art galleries since I was a small child," said Alice. "My parents had me sketching and doing watercolors. They must have many stashed in the attic in Ireland. As I grew older, I used the hobby for relaxation. You're a darling to think I'm good!" Alice hugged Halley. "Of course I needed more brushes and paint colors!"

"It also shows up in your food presentations!" Dory exclaimed.

"We should arrange for you to showcase your work, if you have many more done. Do you want that?" Halley raised her brows.

"I never considered my work as desirable to the public. Over the years, my close friends far and wide have selected from what I completed. You really feel they are worth showing, Halley?"

"Didn't you listen to my report on that one?" Halley asked, disbelieving her.

Dory interrupted with, "Alan and I viewed them for the first time several days ago and thought them marvellous. We don't want to lose Alice, so we kept quiet on our feelings. We were staggered that Alice kept such talent hidden under her bed, in her closet and in the locked storage in the attic."

"Ouch," exclaimed Alice. "How did you locate all the others?"

Dory raises her eyebrows. "Remember our backgrounds, Alice?"

Chapter 21

AFTER THE CARS WERE DESTROYED AT THE DOCK, LLOYD Hardy called Mel Steffes and related the meeting that had taken place. He wanted Steffes to consider escaping to a foreign country for personal safety.

Two days later, after the funerals for those killed in the explosions, Mel Steffes met Hardy at the legal firm after office hours. "The funerals were lavish, just the way the bosses like things! It is time to clear my and Dad's dealings from your office. Hand me all the hard copies you and Jack have. Lynn is gone already. In two days I leave here, and I'll join her in two weeks. There were undercover FBI tracking our connections. We did good business, Lloyd—no hard feelings. I'll wait while you retrieve the data."

"Mel, do you need connections for identity changes?"

"Just forget all about the Steffes. No traces. I have my contacts to work wonders."

"You have a briefcase for the works, Mel?"

"Here, fill it, Lloyd."

Hardy returned with Jack Kendell's files and dropped them into the case atop his own files. "The best to you in the future, Mel. I'll be retiring after all this, too." They shook hands.

After Mel left, Hardy used bathroom Lysol to wipe down all surfaces in his and Kendell's office. He checked for "bugs" in the vents, ceiling lights, plants, and through the bathroom.

In the morning he would dissolve the firm, assigning clients to each of the alternates who would take them. Later he would have a packing company collect and box all their remaining files. A liquidation company could retrieve the file cabinets and furnishings. He would pay a year's salary to the secretaries. He reviewed his plans, looking for any steps he might have missed, before locking the office and the building, and heading home.

Home looked inviting. He showered and changed into casual khaki slacks and T-shirt. In the library/den, Hardy poured a half glass of bourbon and put on a CD of soothing guitars. He contemplated the happenings at the Dock. He had a second bourbon, and eventually decided on an action and retired for the night.

The next day, before going to the office, Lloyd donated twenty thousand dollars to each of four New York charities, "Be Happy" Children, Wheelchairs 4 Kids, Quadriplegic Sports and Society for Disabled Viet Nam Vets.

Hardy met with his legal partners, Ben Hanson and Jack Kendel, in the office conference room. He stated, "We no longer have a contract with the Mob. Mel revealed there were undercover FBI watching us and the Mob. I'm ready to retire quickly. It's my choice at this time. What are your thoughts?"

Hanson said, "Since the Mob cars were blasted to kingdom come, I've been nervous. It makes you think seriously of making a quick getaway."

E.P. STASZ

"If we run this close to that event, we'll look suspicious to the FBI!" Kendel cautioned.

Hardy reminded them to consider the ongoing investigation into Todd's location.

Hanson said, "I can be gone quickly too, Lloyd. I updated my passport last week. I'll find work abroad, maybe Australia."

Kendel shook his head. "We are like rats abandoning ship before realizing they will drown. Lloyd, your stance of leaving due to age is justified. If you have voiced that around in the community long before now, you're set. Do we contact all your clients and give them alternates to use? Lawyers have a bad name; however this action could soften the appearance of fleeing the crime."

Lloyd drank coffee, considering the idea. "Let's contact some alternates, then the clients. I'll write a request we could fax to our chosen alternates. Later Jack can write the fax for the clients, listing the alternates we offer. Emphasize it's the client choice and he/she can also go elsewhere. Ben, try to confirm possible employment before leaving. That action can help avoid suspicion. Okay, let's get to work!"

Back in his separate office, Jack Kendel contemplated their plan. It had been a great ride with the mob! What a bonus to the regular lawyer work! He pulled out the folder of the building lease and studied it. The penalty clause could be easily overridden with a small payment.

He wrote a tentative client letter. Even before Todd's kidnapping, Jack had made plans for terminating the partnership. This office work was boring compared to mercenary work. And then there was Todd—*he must have known something that made him quit us.* Jack had enough funds; with some sporadic work, he would be quite comfortable in his already-chosen Hawaiian beach hideaway. He would check his surveillance equipment after office hours. There would be enough evidence to acquit him, should it be necessary.

Chapter 22

IT WAS NINE O'CLOCK ON THE EVENING OF JULY 5 WHEN A large tourist yacht docked at Halifax, Nova Scotia, Canada. Several of the departing passengers were obviously drunk, assisted by others. They caused some disturbance with their loud, disjointed singing and locating of homeward taxis. Twenty passengers signed in at Sea Side Inn.

Near midnight, two of the sailing crew left the yacht, supporting a weary-looking bearded sailor. At the Sea Side Inn, two rooms were obtained and they retired. Hours later, the night was quiet as the two sailors dressed the exhausted man in rugged jeans and a denim shirt and laid him onto the bed. They put his earned seaman's pay into a worn wallet and slipped it into his pocket. Then they silently slipped back to the yacht. They had been handsomely paid for this duty.

Next day one of the maids found the man still sleeping in the room. She continued to the next room—what a mess! Dirty sailor clothes, dirty food dishes and muddy boots, besides the usual cleanup. *I must tell the boss about this.*

* * *

In Seattle, Matt Neil questioned the two men rescued by Nick Farrell on the hiking trail.

Though kept separated, two hours later they still had the same story—although the sequence was off.

"My name is Peter Wagner, from Vancouver, B.C., Canada My friend is Frank Dumas. We work at Walker's Electric Corporation. Our wives, Emily and Gladys, were killed in an auto crash. We're torn! We decided to hike and get over it. About an hour from Old Man House, we stopped for lunch. Near the end of the meal, we were attacked! Springing from the forest were four bears who pushed us down and hit our heads and punched our bodies. Waking later, I see they looked like hairy mountain men, maybe late twenties or thirties. We hurt, ask for water but instead we're drilled on the names to use. We got hot coffee not suspecting it was drugged. Later we wake, they are gone.

We check around and find only one backpack left and it is missing clothes, food, and three water bottles. In the side pocket there were passports, not ours, licenses, not ours. Our map of the trails and was also gone.

I guessed it might be eleven or twelve o'clock. From what I could remember of the map, ahead was the shortest hike to help. We drank water, and started walking. If we found a creek, we rolled in it and hiked on. When help arrived we were very low. I thought it was St. Peter and an Angel. The hospital in Seattle got us back on our feet and two days later, as we were leaving, the FBI arrested us. Can you help to get us our own passports, social security cards and drivers licenses back?"

While the story was told, two other agents observed and listened in the next room. They had just returned from checking out the facts from Frank's story. When Matt returned from

Peter's interrogation, Agent Scott reported to him, "We were lucky to get to them before leaving the hospital, Matt. Their names, tragedy and jobs check out. The hospital informed us of the bruises and discolored bodies, another check. Could you work with the Canadian Embassy and get these widowers squared? Let's put them into Red Rock Resort. Engage them in bereavement therapy."

"A great solution!" Matt clapped his colleague on the shoulder and returned to inform Peter and Frank they could take an escorted ride into Red Rock Resort to receive bereavement therapy, while waiting for results on their requests.

The men shook hands. "Thank you!" exclaimed Frank and Peter.

* * *

Matt's cell rang—a call to return to his office. There he received an update from the Rangers. The Rangers had pinpointed some likely areas for hiding and the mystery attackers had been found. "Their hideout was well camouflaged," the Ranger reported. "But they had lived in the bush for eighteen months and were getting sloppy. The smoke and cooking smells drew our attention. We caught the four as they ate rabbit, scrambled eggs and bannock."

The search of the cave they were living in revealed a box holding several driver's licenses and passports in plastic bags. They stole these from innocent campers or tour bus passengers, who may have been far away before realizing the personal loss. "We still needed to find out who they were," said the Ranger. "First we processed them as usual. Then the interviews were done. It turns out they defected from Russia six years ago."

By working on ships they had seen many places and when they docked in Port Angel they escaped the ship, hoping to settle down. They worked on fishing boats. The last one refused to pay for all their work and they left that boat. They still had money saved from previous jobs.

They had bearded faces, as did the fake passports they had. They dressed in jeans and T-shirts like everyone else and moved freely, hiking boat rides for free labour. The thought the surrounding area was beautiful. so they bought camp equipment, camping clothes and hiking boots and set up camp. They found the perfect spot—a warm cave and partial old cabin with a creek nearby, lots of free dead wood and animals for food. They got bored sometimes and stalked hikers or campers. Their early goal was to seek immigration status in the U.S. after they fled Russia's oppression.

The FBI Head Office felt that with a debriefing at Headquarters, they could learn what other skills these fellows had. Immigration and Embassy officials would research the issue.

* * *

In NYC, FBI Inspector Core Carter announced that they now had good evidence on the Mob and the legal firm Hardy, Hanson and Kendel, to prosecute them.

One agent reported, "Sir, the legal firm members have split and their whereabouts are unknown. The top NYC Mob bosses have been wiped out., and the direct family of Loren Steffes have disappeared. Plus, the huge auto pileup near the airport wiped out more Mob, most fresh from Italy."

Carter was not pleased to hear that news. "Gone! We can't nail them! And we still have no news about Todd Denver! We aren't letting this go— keep the Mob and the firm members, especially Jack Kendel, on the back burner."

Chapter 23

THE SAILOR LEFT AT THE HOTEL WOKE AT FOUR IN THE morning. He staggered to the bathroom and drank lots of water. Weaving back to the bed, he collapsed on top and sank back into sleep. At seven o'clock, still morning, he used the bathroom, drank more water, and slept again. By eleven o'clock he was more alert. He sat up and checked his surroundings. Nothing was familiar. He rubbed his hands over his bearded face, trying to remember. He recalled many different workers and many languages all loading and unloading boxes on ships. He remembered fishing.

He looked at his body and grimaced. He walked hesitantly to the bathroom and started a bath. Undressing was slow but he finally lowered himself into the hot water. In a few minutes there was a knock at the outer door and a voice calling, "Are you awake?" The action was repeated more loudly. He could not find his voice to answer. Soon a bright-eyed, petite maid walked into the bathroom and was startled to see him there. She stumbled backward: "Sorry. Sorry. I leave now."

He knocked on the wall continuously and slowly until she returned, turning her head away from him and asking, "How can I help?"

"Do I seem familiar? How long was I here?" the sailor asked.

"Not familiar, no. My boss said you came two nights ago with two other sailors, late at night. The room is paid for four more days, including meals."

"Can you get me lots of coffee, and soup with bread?"

"I'll bring it quickly. Stay in the tub. I'll change the bed."

"Could my clothes be laundered?"

"Certainly, I'll take them now." She stooped to pick them up and the wallet nearly fell from the jeans. "I'll check all pockets and empty them here on the counter."

He soaked, looking at the assortment on the counter. He stood, reaching out to grab all and placed them on the floor to see them better. Before he could study them the food arrived. The maid even brought a chair to set by the tub. Again she hurried out, saying, "I'm changing the bed now."

He added more hot water to the tub, relaxing with a good coffee. Then another coffee before concentrating on the soup and bread. After an hour in the tub, his meal eaten, he left the assortment on the floor and returned to bed. He quickly slipped into sleep.

Some time later he woke just in time to vomit beside the bed. Lying back exhausted, he slowly moved his hand to grab the phone but it crashed to the floor. His brain blackened and he passed out.

At four o'clock the concerned maid checked on him again and was distraught when she smelled the mess, then saw the hanging head, hanging hand and the scrambled phone. She told her boss, who contacts an ambulance and the RCMP.

Bill Jewel of the RCMP took the sailor's photo. The paramedics quickly rushed the sick man to Halifax Hospital.

Closely examining the room, Jewel bagged the mystery man's clothes and the bathroom floor contents. He interviewed the maids and the Inn boss.

The petite maid stated, "He seemed confused. Yet he was kind. Now I think he was sick. I told my boss about him."

The Inn manager explained to Jewel about the arrival of three sailors near midnight, July fifth. One prepaid for a week of rooms and food. Only this one sailor had remained at the inn since then.

Jewel inquired, "Where are the man's clothes? None were in the room."

"The maid found dirty sailor outfits and muddy boots in the room adjacent. They went to laundry. She also had this man's jeans and shirt laundered."

"Did she remove a backpack or luggage."

"She only found him and the clothes he wore, that first day she checked. With all the revellers coming from the tourist yacht, it was natural to think he was drunk also."

Jewel collected the man's effects to be examined more closely. The Inn manager collected the other sailors' clothing and handed over the bags.

"What was the name of the yacht," Jewel asked.

" I don't know! Ask the local fishermen."

"Okay. Call me if you receive more information."

* * *

At the RCMP station, Jewel closely examined the worn wallet. It held worn Canadian, American, Italian, and Russian denominations. It was a goodly sum. The man must have been employed for weeks, and not spending. The driver's license name was hard to decipher, as it was water soaked. There was a damaged, faded photo print of a woman. Another jean pocket contained a sailor knife, whistle, and a flat tin with flip top containing three white pills. Everything smelled of fish. No passport.

Jewel arranged to place a guard on the hospital room for the rescued Inn sailor. Then he had his sketcher use the police photo taken at the hotel to draw the mystery man beardless. He assigned a junior agent to go through the convicts' data banks, looking for a photo match. He faxed all the collected information to officials in adjacent provinces and states, and then called another officer to track all docking records in the last week and report back asap.

Jewel then called Dr. Stubb at the hospital. "What's the condition of our latest delivery to you, Doc?"

"Bill, you all saved his life. Blood tests showed he had ingested a lot of opioid drugs like fentanyl. This continuous use causes body trauma. His body isn't starved, so he must have been working in a state of 'taking orders gladly.' The physical work may have offset some of the drug effect. Have you found his identity?"

"No, Doc. We have tracking sent out. Hopefully we get answers. Have the guard keep continual visuals on our man at all times. A nurse must be in the room if the guard needs food or the use of the restroom. I'll arrange for other officers to cover shift changes. That's it for now. We'll talk when more info comes."

"I'll call if there any new changes in our mystery man."

Bill sat back, considering. He phoned his wife Liz to bring him food as he waited for reports. Some missing piece was bothering him—what was it? He worked through some correspondence that had been put on hold since the Inn manager's phone call. The thought flashed! Sailors often had tattoos.

He called the hospital again and asked the head nurse, "Fran, when you were examining that sailor with Doc Stubb did you notice any tattoos? I've had this hunch about sailors."

"We'll get to it, Bill. No quick call means no tattoo. Now eat your dinner, Bill. I know you!"

Jewel's wife, Liz, arrived and set a plate of food beneath his nose—curried chicken, vegetable rice, pickles and chocolate cake. She poured him some of her rich coffee, then sat to to watch him.

When he finished he rose to hug her tightly. "Thank you, gorgeous. I've a mess to sort through tonight."

The phone rings.

Liz packed up the containers, wiggled her fingers at Bill, and left. His phone rang just as the door closed.

"Hi Bill, it's Fran. It is subtly placed at the right inner hip, just below where a man's briefs fit the waist."

Bill is anxious and interrupts "What is it? What? What? "

"It's two inches in length. It has seven stars arranged in the shape of the Big Dipper. So cool! So very cool! I snapped a photo and faxed it to you."

Jewel grabbed the fax and studied it. It certainly looked like the Big Dipper. He faxed the photo to the previously contacted provinces and states. He checked the time: eleven at night already. Time to go home to Liz. Morning should bring results and hopefully solutions for the rescued mystery man.

*   *   *

He hadn't even made it into bed when his agent phoned him at home. "Bill, it's Bobby. Set up your recorder."

"Got it! Give me facts."

"The yacht, named *Galahad*, was a private charter from Boston. The owner lives in London, England—William Burns, Esquire. He also has a large home in Italy. The yacht's Captain is changed about every two months when it's chartered. This recent July, the Captain was Benjamin Rogers, according to the sixteen passengers. They were only aboard for three days and especially for the July Fourth celebrations. It was a grand party with lavish food, lots of liquor, dancing, great fireworks over water and sexy servers. Besides the Captain, there were ten other crew in sailor clothing. I ran a check on Benjamin Rogers and the name comes up deceased in New York. None of the passengers took photos. The other boats in the harbour were smaller yachts and had their own parties and fireworks. They never noticed a tourist yacht. Maybe it was further out."

"In the morning, check with this William Burns, or decide if London Police can first relay us info on him. Good job, Bobby. Get some sleep now!"

Chapter 24

IN NEW YORK'S FBI OFFICE, TWO AGENTS DRANK COFFEE AS they started the early shift. They are interrupted by the sound of the fax machine starting up.

"Hey Royce, look at this!" His colleague waved a sheaf of faxes at him. "Good news! Todd Denver is alive! He's in the hospital, in Halifax, Nova Scotia. Remember when we teased him about the tattoo? Here it is in the photo!"

"Let's read all the faxes, before seeing Inspector Carter," Royce cautioned.

They read carefully. All the faxes had come through the RCMP Halifax office, from Bill Jewel.

"Call Scott Hayes, too—he worked closely with the Denvers," suggested the other agent.

Scott entered the office as Inspector Carter finished reading the faxes. He read them aloud for Scott, exclaiming, "Finally something shakes loose! I'll alert the medical helicopter pilot. Until we learn more, Scott, do not contact Kate/Halley. Instead, notify our hospital to be alert for Todd's arrival today. Everyone, consider the money in his wallet from all those countries—was it planted on him or was he put to work? I'll contact Bill Jewel and hope the patient is ready to leave, and find out if there's a landing pad at Halifax, Hospital."

*   *   *

Hours later, the medical helicopter arrived at Halifax Hospital and two paramedics and Scott emerged. Bill Jewel met Scott and led him through the emergency doors and to Dr. Stubb's office. The doctor had all the medical paperwork completed and handed it to Scott. "You're fortunate that the hotel manager and the maid were quick to seek help from the police and ambulance. It saved his life. It was Bill here who found the clues to his identity."

Scott thanked Dr. Stubb for Todd's care. "The FBI will handle the cost. It's a delicate situation. We'll get back to Bill with details later." The three men shook hands.

By this time the patient was strapped into the helicopter, paramedics attending closely. Scott joined them and they set off to NYC Hogan Hospital.

Chapter 25

THE HOSPITAL ADMINISTRATOR IN BOSTON CALLED THE number provided by Captain Keller and told his employer, William Burns, that Captain Keller was ready for discharge and intended to return to London.

"No," said Burns. "I'm in Boston now and will have him brought here. Let him know to expect a driver in half an hour. Thank you for his care. Fax me his bill, I'll cover it."

In Burns' Boston office, Captain Keller was offered refreshments with hot muffins, cheeses, jam, and fruit.

"I've read the reports, Alan," said Burns. "I'm pleased you were found soon after the kidnapping. Do you remember the men? How many? How they were dressed, or any physical marks? What language they spoke?"

"Two guys. Bearded faces, black knit caps. Black, longer hair. All in black pants, boots, and jacket. They wore gloves. With all my bruises, they might have worn iron knuckles underneath. They were ordinary sized, about four inches taller than me. They never talked. Boss, I'm sorry for the trouble. I don't gamble and feel I never offended anyone. But why steal a ship? I'm baffled.

Have you found the *Galahad*? What about our crew? What happened to them?"

"I discovered that the *Galahad* entertained many passengers for three days, celebrating the 4th of July. The passengers disembarked at Halifax, Nova Scotia. The Coast Guard found the *Galahad* anchored and abandoned near Belfast, Maine. The interior is not damaged. I'm considering selling it. I've placed ads in the media to locate our old crew. Rick, John, Frank have contacted me. They reported their willingness to stay on but they can easily work for others, if I sell. No others called in yet. What would you prefer, Alan?"

"I enjoy employment under you, Boss. On a yacht, or I'd consider something else."

"Thank you, Alan. Hang in there and we'll figure something out. Meanwhile, you're welcome to stay at my Boston house until things are worked out. The butler, Logan, has prepared a bedroom for you upstairs, on the right. Use the kitchen as you like and ask him if you need anything. I feel you need more healing. I must leave and do some office work."

*   *   *

William Burns contacts Inspector Carter at the New York FBI office. "With the *Galahad* and crew being kidnapped, I feel I left you operating solo, Core. What's Todd's condition now? Would it be advisable for me to be with him?"

"Give him three more days. He was nearly dead when rescued in Halifax."

"Has his wife been contacted?"

"No, we're holding off until he functions better."

"I'll meet you in five days, then, around five p.m."

Burns paced his office, contemplating. His Italian mother had left her holdings in Italy to him when she'd died three years before. Two years later, the Mob in Italy had contacted him! They hadn't known of his connections in the U.S. It was wonderful that Mel and Lynn Steffes had managed to slip free. They had changes in identity and passports. *Where are they?* he wondered. Best, perhaps, that it remain unknown! And who had been sent to capture Todd and the *Galahad*? *Todd is resilient,* Burns told himself. *He may have answers.*

Chapter 26

HALLEY HAD SPENT THE LAST WEEK FINDING SECLUDED SITES to photograph, to use later as inspiration to paint, paint, paint! She had gained some weight and her skin had bronzed. If only the FBI would find Todd so her life could be complete again.

She had worried about Jan at the restaurant. Halley had visited and helped cook for two days. Thankfully, Jan now had three new workers that were experienced and happy to work for her. She finally could catch some much-needed sleep and rest her feet. Halley felt safe working out of the way in the kitchen. She was happy to give service to others. On the third morning, Halley presented some photos to Jan, showing her in varied work positions, with candid facial and body expressions. The other workers came to see what made them laugh so much and soon joined in.

Shelley, the cook, said, "Could we make a poster for the customers, Halley? And give originals to Jan. Is that okay with you, Jan?"

"Let me think on it, Shelley. No one ever caught me in the act before! Halley, you are an operator!"

"Ah gee, Jan. I was only sharing your blessings." They hugged and Halley said goodbye to all.

That afternoon, Halley joined Alice, who was using her day off to do some painting. They laughed throughout the day, sometimes sneaking over to paint the other's face, arm, or leg. They talked about many things and Halley again repeated her feeling that Todd was alive and in need of healing. She said healing prayers as she fingered the cat's eye gem often during the painting session. That day Alice produced paintings of people playing volleyball on the beach, and laughing children jumping rope on a lawn surrounded with masses of flowers blazing with color. Halley had completed three paintings and felt pleased with herself. Two held visions of forests, rivers, hawks and masses of wildflowers. The other was a composition of many male faces with different gazes, hair and caps or hats. She felt compelled to paint several young girls' faces on another canvas.

Alice and Halley called everyone to the improvised paint studio. Viewing their work the Yorks, the Farrells, Dory, and Alan were enthusiastic in their praise.

Mike and Trudy grinned at each other. Trudy asked, "Ladies, could we entice you to do a series of paintings for the resort's guest dining room?" Halley and Alice looked at each other and laughed.

"We are serious ladies!" exclaimed Mike.

"Sure," said Alice.

"We'll get back to you on this offer," stated Halley.

Nick looked to Alice, saying, "Why keep your talent hidden? Halley puts her service out to the public under an alias; you could do that too."

"My head is spinning. Later I'll consider it," Alice promised. Changing the subject, she eyed Alan and Dory and asked, "Is dinner ready, cooks?" Dory and Alan had covered the day's food preparations, using Alice's plans and prior preps.

Alan announced, "Come everyone, soup's on!"

"Let's lead them to table," chimed in Dory and they headed for the Yorks tropical gardens.

A long buffet table displayed a tower of flowing, melted chocolate surrounded with fresh fruit and individual sponge cakes. Beside it were platters of grilled chicken, potato and Caesar salads, and cold vegetables.

At the dining table, their glasses were filled with red wine. When everyone was seated, Halley rose with a glass of water and offered a prayer: "From the sweet -scented streams of Thine eternity give me to drink, O my God! I thank Thee, God, for Thy bounties, to possess a radiant heart and a soul open to the promptings of the Spirit."

She paused and smiled at the people around the table. "Everyone clink your glasses and drink. I thank you each for aiding my healing." As she sat, suddenly Ghost jumped on her lap and licked her chin, then leapt down and circled to lie under her chair.

Everyone laughed. Butterflies flitted on and off the table, giving further delight. Conversation poured forth among all the diners.

Chapter 27

AT HOGAN HOSPITAL'S FBI WING IN NEW YORK, TODD DENVER rested his muscled, six-foot-two frame into a cushy easy chair. His curly sun bleached hair with a handsome bronzed face. He was dressed in blue shorts, a blue T-shirt and running shoes, having just finished his therapy session.

Scott Hayes entered the room. "Hello, dear friend. I am very pleased to see you survived."

Todd stood up, smiling, and they hugged tightly.

"Kate never gave up hope for your return, Todd. She offers prayers daily for your healing and return."

"Scott, my good friend! Thank you for coming. Is Kate okay now? It is good to be safe in American hands. Seeing you makes it more real!" He sat down near a table and Scott joined him there.

"How is my Kate? Is she well?"

"I'll give you a short version if you feel you can handle it, Todd?"

"I must get my life back. Will she still love me in my weakened state? Tell me all you know."

"Sure. Hold my hands and look into my eyes, as I relate facts." He took a deep breath and slowly released it. "Here goes. Your flight had a bomb. You were kidnapped. Kate was scared. She packed for flight, disguised herself and traveled away the threat of media, the Mob or your partners. She didn't trust the FBI to protect her, since we did not save you.

Near Seattle, on a bus tour, two elderly brothers, the Yorks, befriended her. They own the Seattle newspaper. She was very tired by then, but still cautious. She asked them for their passport and driver's info, before giving her trust. At their estate in Seattle, the Yorks contacted an FBI friend, Matt Neil, who suggested an identity change. She refused physical changes but accepted the paper trail change. Matt already had a passport and other ID prepared, with her name changed to Halley Coleman. She's been staying at Yorks' and with their friends at the Red Rock Resort near Seattle. Recently she has been doing camera work outdoors and even some painting. She still believes you're alive and in need of healing prayers. That's it! I need some water."

He got up and poured a glass, draining it before he sat by Todd again.

"Considering it? Ask questions." They sat quietly for quite a while.

"Halley after the comet?" Todd mused. "Coleman for the light of the camp lantern? Clever! It certainly suits her. I'll decide whether to become Coleman after talking with her. She is strong spiritually and I'm learning." Todd leaned back in his chair and yawned. "Let's have lunch and I will rest after. The others will be here later. Carter said to leave Halley out of the loop when I report. I'm only to tell her I was on this FBI assignment, because it was involved with the law firm. Thanks, pal."

"As I reported, I felt and saw your old self. That's very good!"

"Is our home safe?"

"It was not damaged. Your friends are living there. We found some loopholes and have it under a company ownership now."

*   *   *

Later the same day, Inspector Carter, Scott Hayes, and William Burns met with Todd in the secluded conference room at the hospital. Todd was pacing the room when they entered. He had changed into black jeans, a black T-shirt, and running shoes. He held a nearly empty glass of water.

More glasses and a pitcher of water sat on the circular table.

Inspector Carter introduced William Burns to the group as they all sat down. Carter explained, "Todd, you were kidnapped and charges will be laid when we know the perpetrator. Your flight was threatened and cancelled. FBI and Air Transportation Safety Commission are investigating. Your law firm was recently terminated, and the whereabouts of the partners is unknown. A week later, the rival Mob bosses, Steffes and Giovanni, were killed in exploding cars. Giovanni had arranged for new family to arrive in New York. They were also killed in a multi-vehicle crash. I know this is a lot to take in—are you following?"

Todd nodded. "Most of it."

Burns asked Todd to report his memories during the "lost" time.

"I was in the terminal hall, walking with my coat over an arm and a briefcase. Suddenly my arm was pinched and I saw a dart in it and tried to grab it but I was falling. When I woke I was on a mattress in the back of a moving van. Some one was watching me, because I was drugged again. Next time I woke up on a bunk on a ship, dressed in sailor clothes. The mates all thought

I was drunk when my "pals" carried me onto to the ship. I was groggy. Didn't know who I was, or where. In my pocket there was an unfamiliar worn wallet with currency form several countries. Oh, and a pocket knife, too. I worked in the kitchen for a while, trying to get my bearings. There was broken English spoken or Italian, or Russian, but nothing I understood.

After eating or drinking coffee, I noticed I was groggy again. I tried to stick to drinking water. Later we reached a tropical port. With the rest of the crew I moved cargo off and brought more aboard. We did that many times. It was exhausting work. There was a bunkmate who tried to be friendly but he was hard to understand. I used the knife to track number of days by my shoelaces.

When I wasn't asleep, I was kept busy working. My brain didn't work well; I couldn't recall my life before the ship.

Maybe days or weeks later, I awoke on a fishing vessel. I worked hauling fish aboard. My footwear had changed. I enjoyed the outdoors! But still I wondered, what was my life before? Who did this to me? Why? Some weeks later, I was back on a cargo ship. Again, not knowing how I got there. This one was Italian. Again we unloaded and loaded cargo. The other bunkmates had quite a sum of money. We played cards and I won some, but days later was drugged again. I always had hope. I had visions of Kate praying for me.

I tried to read the ships' names but I can't remember them. I do recall a yacht, lavish party, lots of tuxedos and fancy dresses and again I was a sailor. My vision became misty. I slept more and walked slowly. One day or night I briefly awoke in a hotel. Somebody helped me to a hospital. Now I'm here. In America. That's good. That's all!"

Carter asked, "Todd, are you feeling good enough to return to working with us?"

Burns interrupted. "Not yet, Carter! Todd, I learned in Italy that some of the new Mob was ready to destroy others and that your London flight was targeted for the Mob members who were aboard. I called Carter and he had the flight cancelled. You were to be taken by the FBI, but others got to you first. I suspect your partner, Jack. Was he a good partner to you, Todd?"

"Jack and I played basketball and tennis in college, that's long before he convinced me to join his firm. They needed my court experience. When I eventually joined the partnership, he was amazed at how my connections made the business soar. He half-joked about being jealous of my success. He did show anger when I beat him at sports. Often he would say, "I'm gonna get you someday." But we discussed how different individuals had weakness and strength in different areas. I told him I had no intentions of taking over his business. He was safe with me. He gave me two weeks' holidays. Hey, I just recalled that!"

William Burns interrupted, "The kidnapping of my crew and the yacht theft were related to Todd's reappearance. The *Galahad* transported you to Halifax, Nova Scotia, leaving you at the Sea Side Inn. That action eventually brought you here. You gave good evidence here. Can we use you again if needed?"

"Agent Burns, at this time I do not know. Am I safe from the Mob? Right now I will concentrate on building my health back. I can't think beyond that—and Kate, I must return to Kate!"

Scott stood. "Todd needs rest again." He took Todd's elbow and asked, "Can you lead the way to your room?"

In Todd's hospital room, a nurse soon entered with two trays of food and medication for Todd. Scott asked for a cot so he could stay overnight. They sat at the tiny hospital table to eat.

E.P. STASZ

Todd wanted more water, and Scott managed to track down ice and a water pitcher.

Scott cleared his plate, watching Todd move his food around but not eat much.

He found some happier news to share. "Red Rock Resort wanted some paintings for their diner and hired Halley and York's employee, Alice. That's what is happening now. Those two are like loving sisters and they paint each other, not just the canvases! Halley sometimes prays aloud as she paints. I'd sure like such a partner... has she any sisters close to my age?" Scott laughed, joined by Todd. "She won't be surprised or shocked to see you again, but you need to call her Halley now."

"Scott, the people who held me, drugged my food and drink to induce memory loss and make me weak. When the effect eased I worked with the crew. I'm thankful they made me work or I'd already be dead. But I need sleep now." He went to the restroom, showered and returned wearing his briefs, and climbed into bed.

Scott found more ice and filled the pitcher again, setting it on the table by the bed. A cot was outside the door and he moved it into the room. He set the food trays out in the hall, staying there to make some phone calls. Finally he, too, prepared for bed.

At two a.m., Nurse Kelly checked on Todd and then contacted the doctor to report her patient's readings.

"We'll return to intravenous plus then. Start it!"

Scott woke as Nurse Kelly finished with covering Todd's chest. As she stood up, Scott was at her elbow.

"What happened?"

"We are continuing his care. Yesterday took much from him, and he's a little dehydrated. He will stay here for a few days yet."

Chapter 28

ALICE AND HALLEY WERE IN A MEADOW SKETCHING, PAINT-ing and photographing. They watched rabbits romping back and forth. Hawks soared high in the air, searching for rodents. There was an abundance of blooming wildflowers. The red craggy cliffs to the side and some swaying trees gave enough contrast to tempt any photographer. In the background the waters of the Puget Sound sparkled.

Halley lay on her stomach, laughing at the antics of the rabbits and snapping shots of their varied poses. She stood and, using an enlargement lens, snapped photos of a deer and her fawns. This was the third film she had inserted into the camera. As she moved downward, she noted a group of dead, broken trees that were still standing and framed them against the red cliffs. She thought, *such great contrasts and yet so natural a setting. Motion surrounded with stability.*

Motion was hers as she rushed from place to place, yet she had lost her stability. She usually thought outside the box; why was she so unfocused now? She sat leaning against a tree and was soon sleeping. Thirty minutes later, she woke and stretched. *Wow! The sun is blazing!*

She slowly searched the horizon, then the cloudless blue sky. She was usually independent. She felt healthy. Why continue being pampered? This thought came out of nowhere. *Wow! O my God I ask Thee, am I finally healed? Is Todd healed? I feel lighter in my spirit and body… it's an uplifting energy. Oh my, Thou art the compassionate, merciful, and beneficent God. Thank you, Lord. Thank you! I feel the healing. Thank you! I can be myself again!* She had hoped and prayed for so long that Todd would hold her again. She would not believe he was gone, but only in need of healing. Faith kept her praying diligently.

She pulled out her cellphone and called her friend Randal—no answer. Then she called Sasha. It rang five times, then a hurried stammer came over the line: "He…hello? Oh, great! It's you, long lost Sister! How are you? I see your number! Yeah! Yeah!"

"I'm so glad to connect again. Is my house still okay? I'm glad my friends are living in it."

"All your friends are good but we are missing you so much, and your loved one. It was hard to return to work, but using your adage "Work lessens worry and brings good thoughts," all of us together began praying morning and night for dissipating any evil that might be following you and Todd. It helped to get us focused. Are you okay now, Kate?"

"Let everyone know my name is now Halley Coleman. I've had an identity change. This is the first time since I left that I've used the phone. Sasha, I had real-live Guardians besiege me in a good way, so my healing will be complete when Todd returns to me."

"You really believe Todd will return?"

"I've prayed daily and really feel in my bones and mind that he just needs healing, but is very much alive."

"You go, girl! We now know prayer can work. We used your Baha'i Faith prayer books and we all pray at the same time. Since I last saw you, I've started working in hairdressing. I had two paintings hanging at the hair studio and they sold to my clients there. Then another two sold to my boss. Cora is back—her boss brought her back to New York to take over half the business, and he gave her an assistant. Adam has added wrestling to the workouts and the clients keep rushing to enrol. He has two new trainers. Randal is in France, doing fashion shoots. He bragged how his charm got the bucks rolling in. He left four weeks ago. He also has another client to start after this gig is finished. When will you return? We miss you!"

"I've only just in the last few minutes realized, I'm not acting independent anymore. I do recognize that this hiccup was needed at the time. But I've started doing some photography and painting, and that must have focused me. There are some important new friends here who have helped me heal. Would it be possible for you to come and visit?"

"Where?"

"I'm near Seattle. Fly in, then find the *Seattle Blues* newspaper office and ask for Sam and Bob York, the owners. I'll tell them to expect you, and they will take care of you all. All for One and Three for All. Whatever works, okay?"

"Sister, I'll get on it. Shall I call back?"

"No. Surprise us."

* * *

Alice was sketching the cliffs, trees, and high above, a bald eagle. She had finished four sketches, making notes about the colors she would use when painting, when suddenly in front of her a

E.P. STASZ

chipmunk sprang from the grass, chattering loudly. She sat still and observed. *Oh, no! That's a snake coming towards me. Can I get away?* A black shadow came over the grass and the eagle swooped down and snatched the snake right in front of her eyes, flying up and up until it landed on a cliff shelf. It deposited the snake there, and soon feathers were flying as the beaks of small eaglets swung parts of the snake from side to side. Alice was entranced.

She heard squirrels chattering in the near trees. They raced across, bounding onto the rocks then back into the trees. The sun shone brightly on a close rock that held a pocket of water, and soon butterflies were darting in and out for a drink. A pair of robins appeared and took a bath. They twitched their fluffed wings until satisfied, then flew away.

What a beautiful day! It took a refugee to show her how much she had missed the outdoors. Sighing, she looked around to see what Halley was doing. Where was she? She stood to get a clearer view, and still saw no sign of the girl. Alice walked upward for better sightlines and spotted Halley far below, by a waterhole.

Alan rounded a cliff corner that opened to the meadow and approached her. "Alice. Alice! How does your garden grow?"

"Oh, Alan. This has been an awakening day for me. There is so much life abounding in the meadow, trees, cliffs, sky and below my feet. I had forgotten these outdoor treasures. Thank God for Halley coming into our life. Do you think Halley will set me up to sell paintings?"

"Okay, what brought that on?"

"I was just going to head over to join Halley, and you come along, right after I had my thinking episode. The stables are close to home, yet I've never sketched or painted the horses or the buildings. Then there are the colors of poultry, their quirks, scratching, and interactions with each other. The dogs will be a challenge, too. I have painted the butterflies and Ghost in many poses. You can come see those. A few days ago Halley critiqued one of my paintings. It was a professional observation. Was I really wanting to hide under a barrel, or could I share? The idea of a show was foreign then, but now that it's stewed awhile in my mind, I've come awake and can embrace it."

"You are a wonder, Alice! As the years come on us, we get wiser, Dad always said. I like the investigative side of the Police or FBI, but would not work full time with them. I fully recognize this fact, yet I like solving problems. The Yorks always keep me in the loop."

"Boo!" Halley shouted, then laughed as she came up to Alan and Alice.

Alice turned and hugged Halley tightly. "You, girl, have awakened my soul. Thank you!"

Alan winked at Halley and stated, "Your magic worked on Alice. However, I came to find you both. It is time to head home."

Halley smiled and said, "My backpack is full of today's work. Alice, need any help with yours? Okay, I'll lead us out."

Alice winked at Alan as they followed Halley.

*   *   *

The Red Rock hosts had invited the York household to join them. Mike and Trudy greet them happily and led them to their home dinner table. A side buffet had a feast spread for all to enjoy. "Help yourselves, everyone," said Trudy.

Dory had come over to help them in their private quarters and to keep an eye on Halley for the Yorks. There were fresh buns, varied cold cuts, cheeses, tofu slices, condiments and hot choices of lobster curry and lasagna, ending with a fruit tray.

Trudy, Dory, Alice, and Halley were grouped at a table in quiet discussion.

Alice looked meekly at Trudy and stated, "I will do a show of my paintings, but Halley must give me tips of how to go incognito, or else all the shopping at the Yorks' will have to be done by someone else."

"Alice, you and Halley did such splendid work for our diner. We receive much praise of the work displayed. I thank you both!"

Alice patted Trudy's arm and said, "Dory and I feel it was Fate that brought this wonderful being Halley to us. She sure paints fast and furious."

Halley was teary-eyed as she asserted, "I have been rejuvenated here, Trudy. I called my New York friends today. It felt right to do that. It's been so long since I used the cell, I had to really think of the number. The Lord does amazing work. One of my friends has more confidence and has started hairdressing. Amid my disaster, bounty comes to my friends. Alice, what a prize you are for me. I believe that sincere, loving actions are what give us the self-esteem to do our best work."

Dory spoke up. "I want you to know, Halley, you have changed us. You have shown optimism all through your time here. Alice is like a butterfly that emerged to first light. I'll be sure she keeps progressing. For myself, you brought out my native singing that I had abandoned. It feels so good to sing again, I'm thinking I might ask the neighbourhood pub to add a weekly performance. It could bring him more business. See, I'm thinking outside the box!"

Chapter 29

SASHA, SAM AND BOB FINALLY ARRIVED AT RED ROCK RESORT. The hostess, Candice, kept up a steady chatter as she showed them all the grounds and treatment centers. Bob observed that many additions had been made since they last stayed. Sasha was very impressed by the facilities.

At two o'clock, Sam rang the office and asked Mike to find Kate/Halley as he had brought her company.

Mike replied, "You come into my home and Halley will be there. She generally returns around this time."

Candice made certain they studied the latest paintings in the diner. "The guests having been raving about them," she said proudly. Sam and Sasha noted A.L. Waters' signature on four of them; the others were by A.T. Swan. They closely studied Waters' work.

"Yup, definitely Sister's work," Sasha beamed. They thanked Candice for the informative tour.

Arriving at the private quarters, Sasha spotted Halley talking with Trudy. Shaking a finger at them was a tiny lady in bright blue slacks and a white short-sleeved blouse covered in printed designs of various buttons. Some were very old shapes and others were from military regimes. She wore her red hair in a bun atop her head. She was now shaking her head, laughing at Halley and Trudy.

Quietly creeping behind Halley, Sasha kept a finger raised against her lips so the tiny lady would be quiet if she spotted Sasha. Reaching Halley, she poked her in the ribs "Boo, Sister!"

Halley squealed, "Sister!" and tightly hugged her.

Halley introduced Sasha all round. Sasha and Alice were soon arm-in-arm, talking like old friends. Sasha grinned at Alice and said, "Marvellous clothes, Alice."

Trudy asked, "Will we all eat together or did you want privacy?"

"We unite with your family and friends, Trudy," said Halley, placing a hand around Trudy's waist as they headed to the dinner table.

They were followed by Alice and Sasha, who started singing, "We are the happy wanderers, travelling the land, to find our sister and her friends, wouldn't that be grand! "

Seated with filled plates, Halley introduced her "sister" around the table. As they ate, Halley related some of the adventures she had had with Sasha, keeping the laughter flowing. Sasha stood to dramatize her rendition of the silent walking, midnight artist and sports personality of Halley, bringing tears to the listeners as they heartily laughed. She continued relating some Halley's disguises, including her changes in language and mannerisms. This kept everyone's laughing attention.

Bob remarked, "We adopted Halley as our daughter. She never mentioned you."

The two girls stood and stated, "All for One. Two for All. We are your daughters!" They raised their glasses, clicked them and drank. Both winked at Sam and Bob.

Alice continued the audience chuckles as she related Halley's antics as they searched for inspiration to do paintings. "Besides, she was an event maker by boosting my confidence in painting. She suckered me into fresh zones by offering some for public sale. Thank you, my friend."

Everyone cheered Alice.

"Well, Sasha, do you have jet lag and need sleep now? We have a room for you—or do you want to bunk together?" Mike asked.

"We will stay together," said Sasha. "Let's go up now. Alice, you come too."

Mike, Trudy, Sam and Bob hugged the girls before they left, thanking them for the entertainment.

Sam remarked, "Halley will be going back with sister Sasha. They sure are happy and lively!"

"These have been entertaining and rewarding days for us, Sam. She is leaving too soon. It just seems too short," Bob asserted.

Trudy states, "I think you're right, Sam and Bob. Yesterday she had a 'shift' in her mind. Dory says her aura is now a happy rose color. Halley has been rejuvenated. Thank you both for bringing her into our lives."

Mike added, "Time to retire, fellows. We'll meet again in the morning."

* * *

In the early morning, Alice and Halley had prepared breakfast. They had eggs baked in bacon rings, hot Red River cereal, fresh fruit, rice pudding and cinnamon buns. Nick was the first up, and he joked with them as the three ate together. He quickly disappeared to lead an executive hiking group.

Sam and Bob asked the new girl lots of questions. Sasha said, "I'm shocked that Halley has not had them dancing, she so loves it! I like to play darts and we invited Halley one night. She had the highest score. Her excuse was, 'my brothers taught me at an early age.'"

"Sasha has painting ability. But she wants a successful man in her life ASAP," Halley laughed.

"Halley forgot her New York sisters and grabbed for new ones. That's okay, because Alice could be a sister to us also."

Sam said, "Bob and I must study the resort's new paintings more thoroughly. Excuse us."

Trudy commented, "Halley has added more vegetarian influence in our diet. I haven't gained weight since she arrived and that in itself is remarkable. I've given the resort chefs some suggestions for changes."

Giggling, Halley admits, "I gave them heck for not promoting health and wellness through the food choices offered. They have the training to lead others but don't practice it. I gave examples of substitutes."

Mike commented, "That was brave of you! I hope it moves them!"

Hugging Halley and Sasha, Trudy and Mike gave their farewells and blessings. They left to catch Sam and Bob. Bob was shaking his head and laughing as Trudy arrived. "These paintings by Waters have many hidden messages. Wonderful surprises!"

"Do you know the painter, Bob?"

"No. Trudy. It is the first time I've encountered such work. Is he local?"

"Sam, do you know the painter?"

"The way you ask, Trudy, it seems we should." Mike and Trudy laugh.

"Considering your delight, would it be Halley?" Bob guessed.

"Yes! The other wall is Alice. We are very pleased to have their work. We will keep Halley's secret."

"Sam, we better get the ladies home. Thanks for your hospitality, Mike and Trudy. We will keep in touch."

Chapter 30

IN NEW YORK, THE TRAVELLERS RETURNED TO THEIR careers. Halley was at the door to Cora's office to join her for lunch when Adam appeared around the corner. He beamed as he spotted her.

"When did you return, Kate?"

"This is the third day. It's difficult to pick up the pace. Join us for lunch?"

"Always a pleasure to join the beauties."

Cora came onto the street as Sasha appeared. They walked to their favourite Japanese take-out, picked up the food order and walked across the street to meet Adam and Halley in the park. It was wonderful to share with friends, Adam thought. "Has anyone word from Randall lately?" he asked.

Cora spoke up. "I had an email yesterday. He's still in France, happily working and eyeing the pretty girls. He has been dancing most evenings with some of them."

Kate said, "Remember, everyone, call me Halley now. How is your business going, Adam?"

"Our friends here, gave you some idea of how we were influenced by prayer? It worked, cause you are back, and we have increased focus at work. Do you still believe Todd is returning?"

"Oh, yes! I had such an uplifting of energy after I called Sasha to come for me. I never doubted he was still alive. My heart feels intact, not broken. Keep saying healing prayers, that is what he needs. I want to thank you all for helping to guard my home after I left. That episode in my life is over, and it is time to move forward. By the way Adam, have you found your love mate yet?"

"Not yet, but I think it could happen soon. I've had a dream in the last few days that keeps repeating. She wears a smashing purple outfit and is a statuesque figure, with blue-black long hair and legs that have no end. It's so real that I wake drenched and need to take a cold shower. He raises his arms, pleading. "When, Lord, will you bring her to me? When? When?"

"I think you need a special holiday, Adam. Go to Ireland where the saints turn ordinary folk into fairy dreamers with the second sight," Halley bantered. They all laughed.

Cora stood up. "Well, we ordinary folk must return to work and let Fate step up to do the soul matching."

Again they laughed, making their way back to work.

At home, Halley set up three canvases and backwashed them. She turned the lights low and then meditated. Nearly an hour later, feeling refreshed, she drank some ice water, set out her gear and started dribbling paint onto her palette. She worked at a frantic pace, her arm movements smooth but quick. When the first canvas felt complete, she plunged on to the next. The force would not lessen. She felt outside herself as she brushed on paint so quickly, like an angel with a feather touch.

On and on she worked, brushing the sweat from her brow and leaving streaks of paint there. Suddenly she grabbed the water and drank deeply. She got another bottle and again emptied it. She sat and breathed deeply for several minutes, then stood and returned to her canvases, finishing the second and moving right on to the third as though the two were connected. Her arm moved more slowly as she kept adjusting shadow, light, and darkness on the canvas. Hours later she felt the sense of completion that told her they were finished. Collecting all her gear, she quickly cleaned the area and equipment.

Turning the light off, leaving the fans on, she left the room and locked it. Sliding the bookshelves across the doorway, she locked them into place. She showered and went to bed. It was midnight!

*   *   *

Four days later, Halley and Sasha broke into Adam's apartment. They carried in her paintings, hoping not to be detected, since they drove a van with a painter stencil. Their hair was tucked under painter caps and they wore painter coveralls to complete the disguise. After all the paintings were inside, they cleaned his living room wall, measured three times, then pounded in six nails for the three. Carefully adjusting to make the paintings level, they hung the new paintings. Then sitting back and viewing them, they hit high fives.

"Why the name change?" asked Sasha.

"It came to me the next morning. I wondered about it at first, then saw the wisdom of it."

Proceeding to the kitchen, they made tea and devoured their packed sandwiches. They laughed as they considered what

Adam's reactions might be. They cleaned everything and left his prior wall decor atop his bed. Bundling their hair under the painter hats, they were ready to leave.

As Halley drove the van into her garage, Sasha got a call on her cell and stated she had to get home in a hurry.

"No worry, Sister. Just change the coveralls and dress properly before you leave. I know how to store this gear."

Sasha scurried into the house and was shortly in her car and driving away.

Halley removed the coveralls and hats and folded them to store in a plastic tub. She removed the truck painter decal. Upstairs she darkened the bedroom, undressed, showered and tucked into bed. She slept deeply, with no confusion and no visions, until five hours later dreams began weaving through her mind.

She soars like an eagle, overlooking dense evergreen forests and sparkling water that tumbles over waterfalls. There are meadows holding many horses and others have herds of deer. She hears and sees birds, butterflies and bees abounding over acres of waving wild flowers that emanate their fragrances. Peace and tranquility reign here. Man should learn from this. Rays of sunshine come into view, followed by rain that gets more and more heavy until it becomes a lashing storm with high winds. This finally slows down and reveals sick children in hospital. She sees the purple auras surrounding two children and begins praying for the healing touch of Spirit to reach all these innocents. The vision changes to ships on sea. Men are carrying big boxes onto a ship.

Much later, she gradually awakened and stared at the ceiling—a blue and green sky vision dotted with varied cloud formations. Sitting up, she saw it was three a.m.

From the closet she took one of Todd's T-shirts and slipped it on. She held the cat's eye gem, knelt and prayed for his safety and return. In the kitchen she made a veggie-loaded omelette and steamed some shrimp. She drank herbal tea. Eating, she considered what she had accomplished in these last days. Sasha was a loyal conspirator. *How else can we help Adam? All us girls should unite in meditation and search for Adam's love mate.*

Outdoors it was dark, no moon glistening the earth. She made a list for her next actions, then booted up the computer to put some actions into the capable hands of others. When the others had accomplished her requests, she would receive confirmation via photo emails. The action that would please the kids most was the clown entertainment. She returned to bed and quickly fell asleep.

* * *

At noon the next day, Halley was sketching in the living room when she got a call from a joyfully excited Adam. "I couldn't wait longer to phone you, Halley. Your talent shows my dream mate. How did you possibly capture her image? Never mind. I'm so very pleased, very pleased. It was a bit shocking at first, I must say. Then I figured the identity of Eva Storm. You sure are sneaky, but in a good way. Thank you again! I have a client now. See you soon."

Chapter 31

SCOTT DECIDED TO TRACK HALLEY. HE CONTACTED SASHA. "Have the sisters hidden Halley? She isn't answering my calls or emails."

"We have been busy. No, we have not made her disappear."

Scott quickly interrupted, "How do I locate her?"

"You're FBI, figure it out!"

"Okay then, meet me at seven tonight at your favourite Japanese restaurant. I'll buy for all her friends."

That evening, Adam teased Scott about his lack of tracking skills, making the girls laugh. Cora started teasing Scott. He was becoming flustered and realized that maybe if he admitted he failed, they would give him some clues.

Sasha exclaimed, "When you see her, say thanks. She prayed and had other FBI agents searching for you a month ago. She only recently made it back here, after twenty-four days of running away. There's only so much time in a day, and she's had a lot to settle. Come on now, let's enjoy this food. Then we go dancing."

"Excellent idea for after the meal. Thankfully, Scott is a good dancer," asserted Adam.

"I've been on heavy assignments these last two months— give me some relief, you guys!" laughed Scott.

The friends clinked wine glasses, smiling at Scott.

"I'll drive you all in my car," Adam said. "Scott can pay our admission, right, buddy?"

"Sure, new friends of mine. I'll treat you."

After arriving at the dance bar, the girls flirted with Scott and kept him dancing. He was even willing to line dance when it started. Drinking and dancing, they were all happy. Hours later, Scott thanked them for the enjoyable company and a good workout. He presented each with his card, hoping they would think of him when again going dancing. He was hoping one would call with information about Halley. They headed home, in cabs.

Chapter **32**

HALLEY WAS AT THEIR CABIN IN THE CATSKILL MOUNTAINS. It was splendid observing the hawks, eagles, deer and fox. She prayed, hiked, slept, snacked and took photos. Occasionally she sketched. When she was refreshed and ready to return to her friends, she called the pilot to pick her up.

She was just leaving the forest when the helicopter arrived—and then almost immediately lifted off again. She was not shocked to see the only man who had brought first thunder and lightning, then rainbows into her life. She had a stubborn and absolute belief that Todd still lived.

Hope. "The thing with feathers that perch on the soul and sings without words and never stops" was how Emily Dickinson said it.

Then she was running to him, tears running down her face. He caught her and hugged tightly. Drawing back, he wiped her tears and slid a hand behind her neck and bent to kiss her. She trembled. Her mouth softened under his. He sensed her rising heat. She was in his arms again, and that was all that really mattered. He led her to the near boulder and sat, bringing her onto his lap. They were both weeping.

She looked into Todd's eyes and whispered, "*Banzai*, my one and only, Todd."

He kissed her eyes, her cheeks and murmured "*Banzai*, forever and always, my Halley."

The Japanese greeting that translates, "May you live 10,000 years," had become their own private lovers' greeting.

As the cold settled around them, Todd said, "The pilot will return in four days. Love, let's go in. I need you desperately!"

She looked in his eyes, clutched his hand and stood. He stood with her and tightened his arm at her waist. At the cabin door, she punched in the code to unlock it. As the door opened, Todd lifted Halley and carried her across the threshold, kicking the door shut behind him. He lead her upstairs and they renewed their passion through the night.

* * *

The next morning, after coffee, sausages, pancakes and more coffee, they went hiking. By the waterfall he held her close and told her everything that had happened to him.

"Love, I felt you praying for me, Kate. That kept me going. There was a shift as time passed and you were disguised, but it was surely still you, Kate. When I debriefed with Scott, he spoke of your new name, Halley. Your feathers of hope reached me. Thank you, love. Thank you, my Halley! "

Comfortable in their love for each other, holding each other tightly, they exposed their emotions and sobbed.

"Halley, tell me of your travels while I was gone."

"The day you left, I realized my paintings had become violent in color. I had returned from my run when Scott called. He said that someone kidnapped you. He had a company set up security cameras throughout our yard. But mob business is brutal, and we also thought maybe your firm was the problem. I couldn't risk bringing harm to our friends or family. And the media bombardment would devastate me. So I loaded up my backpacks and ran away. I met a women, Andrea, in Baltimore, and she sensed that I should stay near water, forests and animals. I bus toured through a series of parks, ending in Cleveland. That was day twelve, and still no word from Scott. I flew to Yakima, Washington. On another bus tour, we had a breakdown at Tacoma. Two older men, the Yorks, rescued me—Todd, I was so exhausted by then! Between them and the Red Rock Resort I was comforted. I prayed and prayed for you. I had Sasha and my other friends pray at the same time of day for us. Thank God you have returned!"

"Thank you. I can recall your journey with the helpers to offset my nightmares. I love you, sweet wife of mine. Never forget that!'

Halley smiled up at him. "Come, love, my one and only Todd. We must walk and enjoy our new day. Hiking outdoors brought me balance. Eventually I began to paint again. When I felt lighter in spirit, I knew you were in a good place again. It was belief in prayer that returned you to me. Now we put all that in our past and walk forward into our future. The fishing poles are behind that boulder and guess what's for dinner?" They laughed. Holding hands, they ran to the stream and fished for their dinner. Later, taking their fish to the cabin, Todd remarked, "We must delight in the simple wonders of God's handiwork!" Halley squeezed his hand.

E.P. STASZ

Chapter **33**

RETURNED TO THEIR NYC HOME, TODD WALKED THE BACK-yard, stopping near the waterfall to look back at his home. "Lord, thank you for bringing Halley into my life before the chaos. See this beautiful space we created. Focusing on this and her spirituality, I am truly blessed. She never gave up that I was alive. Thank you, Lord, for giving her strength and giving her helpers in her distress—yet she was reaching out to help others. She often comments, 'Pay it forward.' I shall keep that motto too!" He returned to the house with springy steps.

Halley and Todd often walked the shore where they first met. They played tennis at the club and were often invited to play against others. He accepted a program of training at Adam's fitness center. She even had Todd go bowling, where they met more new people. Randall, Sasha, and Cora came to dinner often. Todd was rejuvenating.

* * *

Fred Nader and Scott Hayes were visiting them. Conversation was interrupted by the loud telephone answering machine.

A disguised, muffled voice stated, "Partner, I am ashamed that the prank took a devastating turn. I placed some sums into your account to ask for forgiveness. You knew of our work with the M's and I'm running from them. I'm sorry about the kidnapping. You were the star of our firm and I envied your success. You even had a great marriage. It was not fair. I hate to give up tropical bliss, but I'm gonna wear fatigues again."

When the call came in, Halley had risen but Todd pulled her to him, whispering, "I think it's my old business partner, Jack."

Scott inquired of the hosts, "Do the expressions bring someone to mind? Regardless, I'll have the phone company trace it." Using his cell, he put that into action.

Todd shuddered, then said, "Scott, Jack Kendel was a mercenary before he went into law and 'the M's' relates to the Mob bosses. It seems *he* was behind my kidnapping. Scott, can you disperse the funds he is talking about into shelters and charity cases? Let's work from my office. Fred, please stay with Halley?"

"Todd," said Halley, "check my account in case he was fudging it also."

"Right love, I'll be back with Scott in a few minutes."

"Todd, don't be alarmed," said Scott. "We have trackers on the new Mob bosses. Jack may have transferred the funds to you for the Mob to trace. Consider: do we track Jack for the FBI to prosecute him?"

"Here's my account—let's take a look. Our government should not hire him or let him return to the U.S."

"Whee, it's more healthy now! My handy book says seven local charities and six women's shelters. We will route it to the Cayman Islands, then Las Vegas, then to the charities. How about donations to the thirty local schools and to disabled veterans, Todd?"

"Do whatever to release it from me."

Fifteen minutes later, Scott had routed all the money.

Halley appeared in the doorway. "Now check mine, Scott. Here's the account."

"I know you guys can do this yourselves, but with high emotions you make mistakes."

"Looking safe babe, nil has changed since your last entry," said Todd. "You should keep an eye on it for at least a month. Jack is a sneaky character."

Back at the kitchen, Todd, asked everyone to sit. He poured all but Halley a stiff drink. They clinked glasses and Halley asked Scott to explain why they acted as they had.

"Fred, you happened into this event. Halley did not know that Todd's law fiirm that dealt with Mob money. Neither did Todd, when he joined them. The FBI did. The FBI approached Todd to discover the details of their dealings. Todd's former partners took kickback money as they laundered the Mob money. Todd collected this information and informed us, but shortly after he disappeared. Both Mob bosses were killed a week later. The law firm was dissolved after the Mob bosses were killed and the other partners disappeared." Scott paused to take a sip of his drink. "This phone call came from Jack, one of the legal partners. He implies he is the one who had Todd kidnapped and put to work on the ships. Todd was missing for four weeks because of Jack. Now Jack has put money in Todd's account, ostensibly as an apology—and that could make him a target for the Mob. So we got rid of it right away and turned it into a blessing for all the organizations we gifted."

The phone company returned Scott's call with the results of the trace. Todd, Halley and Scott peruse it. There were incoming calls from Khartoum, Sudan also Bogotà, Colombia. The numbers were blocked for both.

"I was hoping Jack would call once we had your land line reconnected. Keep track of all calls coming in, Todd and Halley. It may give us clues as to Jack's location. The FBI will continue to track the new Mob bosses as well." Scott turned to Fred. "Mr. Nader, please keep tonight's visit to yourself."

Fred took Halley's hands, saying, "I understand why you left suddenly, but you're back now and when you or Todd need help, count on me." He said to Todd, "Take a rest to heal well. If you would like to work in construction for a bit, I can place you in position. Stay healthy, happy and prosper, Todd and Halley."

Todd said, "Scott, we appreciate your work with us. Halley and I are going to return to the cabin for two weeks."

"Did Jack know about your cabin?"

"Not that I remember. Being with Halley outdoors will help me heal better than therapy."

After Scott left, Halley wanted to discuss their plans with Todd. "Instead of the cabin, we could go to the Red Rock Resort in the Seattle area. There are many trails, lots of workshops, forests, cliffs, and water."

"You suggest this so we can seek a new future and escape the past?"

"Perhaps. I mostly wanted to keep us interacting with people, yet still be in the spectacular outdoors. They have canoes, sessions of Ti Chi, Yoga and Meditation, to name a few. I'll stay with you for what you choose to do."

"All right love. I need you close. We can go to the resort. Let's pack now."

"No rush, Todd. We'll just need one backpack each. Let's see, you'll need runners, toiletries, dress shoes, socks, one dress pant with shirt, four tops, shorts, jeans, swimsuit, and gym suit."

Todd grabbed her, giving her a whisker rub. "Minx! I can be selective, lets pack now!" He rushed upstairs.

"Maybe we can buy the dance outfits," Halley said after catching up.

Todd already had a pile stacked on the bed: shorts, briefs, socks, collected toiletries and shoes, a shirts, jeans, and a pair of dress pants. He swiftly brought the backpacks and started stashing.

"Lord, you really want to travel, Todd."

"Stay to the plan, love. That works for me right now."

Halley quickly put garments and shoes in her backpack. She tucked water bottles in the side pockets. Her handbag held Baha'i books, toiletries, and her camera, sketch pad, and pocketbook.

Chapter **34**

ON THE FLIGHT, TODD SLEPT RIGHT AWAY. HALLEY SPENT about an hour sketching and snapping pictures of him and some of the other passengers. The she, too, slept.

A rental Jeep was waiting for them when they landed in Seattle. Halley had phoned the Yorks earlier and spoken to Alan, who had insisted they must stop for the night and have dinner with them.

"I won't say a word—we'll surprise them. I'll assist in the kitchen. See you soon, Halley and mate!"

As they arrived at the Yorks' estate, Todd squeezed her hand. "Love, I fully understand. It is serenity."

They parked and Halley walked Todd through the land-scaped grounds to the stables and talked to the horses.

"Love, did you feel you were guided to this place? It is so You!"

She hugged him tightly. "God works in mysterious ways. I meditated and the healer I met in Baltimore confirmed it. When I fled, Cora, Sasha and Adam purchased Baha'i books to say prayers for both of us. They were rewarded. They did not believe earlier when I said prayer helps. Let's head to the house."

Arms around each other, they walked through the food garden and Halley explained the natural watering system the Yorks utilized. They taste samples of the vegetables. At the back door leading to the kitchen, Halley quietly opened the door and stepped, in seeing Alice, Dory and Alan finishing the dinner preparations. Holding onto Todd she shouted, "BOO!"

The three shout "Yikes " " Your back! Thank you Lord. "

Alice grabbed onto Halley and hugged tightly, tears rolling down her cheeks.

"My, my, it's raining in my kitchen! And this is the magic man, Todd. Look at you! No wonder she held on for your return, handsome man." Todd took Alice's hands and kissed her knuckles. Alice stepped back. "Meet these others Todd—Dory and Alan."

Dory hugged Halley, exclaiming, "Your aura is radiant like a rainbow! Todd, you are her soul mate. She would not let you go, handsome man." She winked.

Todd took her hands, kissed her knuckles and holding them, inquired, "What is my aura, friend to Halley?"

"You have seen sunsets? It is pastel golds, pinks, and mauve. Your wife is back and life can begin anew... I'm so pleased for you both." She stepped back and Alan came forward.

He shook hands with Todd and asked, "May I hug your wife, Todd?"

"Does the butler, advisor and nurse need to ask? Hug! All three of you kept her safe for me."

Alan hugged Halley and said, "No wonder I did not impress you. Todd is a keeper!"

Laughing, Halley states, "You're wonderful, Alan. But my heart was already in Todd's hands and I never noticed another man. Are the Yorks in house?"

"Yes. Go to the library. We will complete the dinner."

At the library door, Halley said to Todd, "Sam and Bob rescued me at the low point of my journey. She opened the door and, holding Todd's hand, entered the room. Sam and Bob were at their desks and quickly stood, smiles beaming.

Bob said, "Hallelujah, our daughter has returned! Give us some hugs, friends."

Sam declared, while shaking Todd's hand, "We hoped to see the man who captured Halley's heart. Todd, we are so pleased to have you with us. We adopted your wife as our daughter."

Todd hugged Sam. "She is my soul mate! Thank you, Sam." Todd moved to Bob and hugged him, saying, "Thank you, Bob. The Lord had you rescue my wife and brought her health back. I am thankful. What can we do to repay you?"

"Todd, you have returned and it makes Halley whole again. That is our payment. Come have dinner with us." Sam led them to the conservatory.

Halley interrupted. "Excuse us, Sam. Todd needs to roam the tropics first."

In the tropics room, Ghost was soon weaving around Halley's feet. Laughing, she picked him up and stroked his head, throat and back. Ghost purred. She set him back down, and holding Todd's hand, wandered along. Butterflies were flipping around the pair, with Ghost happily following Halley. Later, when Todd saw they were near the end, he halted, embracing his wife. They smiled, gazing into each other's eyes.

Everyone was seated when they returned. "Come, join us and fill up," said Bob.

The buffet featured roast salmon with lemon sauce, rice pilaf, mixed bean salad, a platter of sliced vegetables and a tray of fresh fruit.

Sam said, " Todd, I invite you to visit the newspaper. We are an excellent resource for students from the local college to learn how to do research. Lawyers as well as detectives should make more use of the newspaper resource."

"You have a passion still for your chosen profession, Sam. Bob feels the same?"

Bob nodded. "Had we not the habit of researching in the field, Halley would not be known to us. Did she explain what happened?"

"Yes, she explained, Guardians and friends. We are taking life more slowly for now. United at last, we agreed to move forward. Releasing the past will come in time. I debriefed with the FBI. Now I will focus on me and mine."

"When Bob and I lost our wives to illness, we were distraught. At the Red Rock Resort, we had bereavement counselling. Halley rejuvenated with painting, sketching and photography. She convinced Alice to share her art. Alice is quite proficient, but she kept it hidden until Halley encouraged her. Now she has gallery shows. She's tickled that others find them wonderful."

Sam, Bob and Alan went for dessert. Halley left the others and clutched Todd's hand. He hugged her.

She asked, "Shall we retire soon? This is a lot of newness for you."

"After dessert will be a good time to make our escape, my Halley." She squeezed his hand. He placed their entwined hands on his heart and kissed her.

*   *   *

Later in bed she said, "Love, in the morning sleep as long as you like. I might be up earlier and take a run. I'm back to normal, observing sunrise and sunsets. Ohhh, it's so good to have you back!" She wiggled tighter against him and he tightened his hold.

"Do others know where you run?"

"When I stayed here, one was always watching me, I learned later. Alan rides horses and saw me running. There's a high point in the land near the stable, where you can see both sunrise and sunset well."

"This household loves you well, my Halley. The women and Alan were keeping you in conversation so Sam and Bob could grill me."

"When they first encountered me, they said, "We have one hundred and some years of experience" and that they could help me." They had sincere eyes, and I was trusted them. When I reached this place, the home vibrations settled me down. I began relaxing. Remember the conservatory, I slept there a lot when healing. There is a comforter under the bench." Halley yawned. "Let's sleep now. We eat breakfast in the alcove in the kitchen."

"Love, did my absence affect your art skills?"

"When I ran, I only took a small camera. Much later I started painting. My skill is fine."

Todd ran his hands over her body, watching her face as they roamed. He kissed her eyes, nose, and throat, nibbled on her ears and onto her sweet lips. She pressed her palm against his heart, noting the beats matched hers. His need pounded through him, focusing at the back of his neck, roaring in his brain and dulling his senses. Her body flamed for him. He rubbed circles on her breasts then placed his mouth on each in

E.P. STASZ

turn, tonguing her sweet essence. His hand was igniting passion in her private place, making her rise upward. She was wet and hungry. He flipped back, her body covering his, stroking to give her vast pleasure. Power swept over them. They were drunk and lost in each other. Finally sated, they slept, holding tight.

*   *   *

Halley and Todd spent four days with the York household. Halley could see the strength building in her husband. The toxins were clearing from his system. Far away from the old life, he was becoming more settled and comfortable interacting with peoples. They rode the horses, picked fruit, ran two miles a day, joked with Alan and teased Alice and Dory. Alan and Todd visit the local pub and heard Dory singing her Irish tunes. The three had a good time with the locals.

He was a varied lover each night to his one and only Halley.

Chapter **35**

IT WAS TIME TO HEAD TO RED ROCK RESORT. JUST AS NICK had done for her first visit, Halley had Todd halt at the lookout. Todd sat on the bench and Halley gave him a bottle of water and an orange while they admired the views. Twenty minutes later, a tour bus pulled in behind the jeep. The pair returned to their car, holding hands. Arriving at the resort, they encountered an excited Phil and Beth.

"The baby is on its way!"

Phil quickly drove away. Mike and Trudy were not home. Halley showed Todd the private conservatory.

Todd asked, "My love, do you want one in our home?"

"I never gave it a thought, Todd. We can talk about it when we get home."

"It is interesting that the Yorks have one too."

"They are both different, Todd. Here there are parrots, and gorgeous orchids." But Halley had something else on her mind. She turned to him. "Todd, when the FBI had you in hospital, I felt a lightness in my heart. Even though they hadn't yet contacted me, I felt ready to return to our home. Scott gave me dates and—is it coincidence our calendar dates match?"

"Love, we are soul mates! We are deeply connected! Our hearts pump in unison!"

Before opening the door into the public area, Halley embraced her one and only Todd. Minutes later they entered the Red Rock Resort area. To the right was the large kitchen. Several workers caught sight of Halley and waved, and she waved back. Moving on, they entered the empty diner. Todd placed an arm around his wife and headed to a painting. Examining it, he looked at his wife and said, "This is not yours."

"Correct you are, my love. Alice releases her pent-up energy, an Irish trait, by painting!"

"You stand here. I'll come back when I've viewed each." He glided to the next, studied it and moved on. Later, after all have been examined, he beckoned to Halley.

Standing before the painting he believed was hers, he said, "This artist hides faces in the cliffs, grass and waterfalls, even sometimes in the clouds. The next two paintings have camouflaged faces also. The artist is A.L. Waters, alias for my wife." He grinned at her.

"Todd, you know me well! Know when I paint, I'm usually in a trance. When finished, I place a prayer for health, happiness and prosperity on the viewer and owner who has the 'eye.' They should be able to quickly see into and feel the movement in the painting as I intended. I detach myself from them, knowing this can happen. You have always felt and seen—that is why I connected with you so quickly when we met at the stormy beach."

"Remember when we joined hands and felt sparks? My intuition was that you did the paintings in my home and in the cabin. I courted you slowly, to convince you that I was for you and you were for me."

They embraced. The sound of applause startled them, and turning, they saw Mike and the two resort chefs.

"Congratulations! Halley has reunited with her love Todd, and I am a grandpa!" Mike moved to them and encircled both in a hug. Teary eyed, he looked at Halley, saying, "Welcome home, and welcome to your husband, Todd."

"Todd this is Mike, owner of this resort. Congratulations Mike. Is it a boy or a girl?"

"Both! A big boy and a smaller girl ! We are twice blessed! Now, we must feed you. Come back to my home." He took Halley's hand to guide them.

In the home dining area, Trudy was waiting for the pair. "Welcome home, Halley and Todd. It is good to see you both so radiant! It is a blessing that you returned, Todd. Mike told you our news of the twins? Good. Let's have some food."

"Trudy, meet Todd, my hero returned!"

"Goodness, I'm flustered, not introducing myself. I'm glad to see your auras are happy halos. Welcome Todd, never be a stranger here."

Mike interrupted, "We need food now! The chef left us plenty."

The buffet was piled high with biscuits, a variety of salads, seafood divan, herbed chicken, fruited wild rice pilaf, a plate of condiments, a cheese board and fruit tray, with whipped cream and a pot of dark dipping chocolate. The beverage selection included assorted juices, water, and yerba mate, an energy-boosting herbal drink.

The dinner conversation grew even more lively when Nick entered. He greeted everyone and sat by Halley, saying, "Lucky you. Your love has returned! Can you get Sasha to return here?

She needs to meditate and hike: perhaps you can suggest she do it here?"

Halley looked Nick in the eye and said, "You're a slow mover. Why did you not show your interest when she was here? I'll help—but have you, by chance, met or seen a tall, striking woman with long black hair, here or in Seattle? A woman like an Amazon?"

Mike and Trudy started to speak together: "At the hospital. A nurse. Today, Nick? "

"Sure, she is an Amazon. I'll get her name and particulars by tomorrow night. Todd and Halley, stay here awhile. If I convince her to come here, you will see for yourself! Who is looking for her?"

"Back home, we have a good friend who needs such a woman. He runs a successful fitness gym. A handsome athlete, who loves to dance and play sports. Don't reveal that to her. Ask what she looks for in a mate, and compare to what I've stated. Does it match? Bring her over here for a visit."

"You want me to be a sleuth? Works for me! How about this—you could bring your camera and take pics of my new niece and nephew."

"We'll see how to fit that in. But excuse us all for now, it's time for us to finish the day."

"Certainly, Halley," said Trudy. "Take the room you had before, it is ready for you and Todd. It is a pleasure to meet you, Todd." Mike echoed her sentiments.

Ascending the stairs, Halley hurried Todd, saying "Trudy will explain these dream hoops tomorrow."

"Let me shower and then to bed, I feel it today! Tired out, yet good."

"Sorry, we moved too fast for you. I can rest now too!"

While Todd showered, Halley spritzed lavender and eucalyptus on the bed linens, and placed a pitcher of lemon water on the end table near where he would sleep. She closed the drapes and adjusted the air conditioner. They would sleep deeply.

Chapter 36

AT BENNETT AIRPORT, SCOTT HAYES, AND THE PRIOR Portland hikers Sheila and Jill, were in the same area yelling for a taxi. One stopped abruptly beside the two women and they quickly moved to it, telling the driver, "Take us to the Red Rock Resort."

Scott heard "Red Rock Resort" and shouted, "I'm heading there also. Let's ride together."

Sheila turned, noticing Scott and said, "Name the owners and a guide?"

Scott laughed, stated the names requested and explained he had been visiting them a lot in recent months. The suitcases were placed in the trunk, while the riders slipped into the backseat, with Scott between the girls. Discovering they were repeat guests, he inquired what they would be doing.

Jill exclaimed, "Last time we badly needed stress relief. We hiked, kayaked, swam and hiked some more. Now we are planning to take Ti Chi and Meditation sessions."

Sheila added, "We are here to build our skills, to allow us to do self and group stress relief where we live. You said you see the Farrells often—has Beth delivered her baby yet?"

"Yes! A boy and a girl. She needs help to raise them. I reminded Phil, her husband, there would be little sleep for the next two years. They would need to sleep when the babies slept. I can hardly wait to witness the household now!"

Jill inquired what career work kept Scott going. He laughed, "Ladies, I am a criminal detective!"

"Humph," said the girls.

"I am a legal accountant," offered Jill.

Sheila inserted, "And I am a legal executive" with a laugh.

"We've arrived!" Scott observed. "I'll pay for the enjoyable taxi ride. See you later, ladies."

As their taxi was leaving, another rolled up, depositing Nick and a remarkably beautiful, athletic woman dressed in a purple skirt set. She had long, blue-black hair and a graceful bearing. Nick shook hands with Scott and introduced Shannon Speers. Scott moved on.

"This is an awesome place, Nick. It must take a bounty of energy to operate," said Shannon.

"We have trained employees. Besides hiking, we offer many classes."

"Let's go, Nick. I must check on the infants. Lead the way." She slipped her arm through his. Nick took her to Phil and Beth's suite upstairs. Finding Beth and the babies sleeping, Shannon tiptoed to the crib for a peek, and then quietly left the room.

Nick was looking beyond the living room window. "Shannon, see the couple over there by the big oak tree? He's a lawyer who was kidnapped and missing for weeks, and is now recovering from the drugs used on him. Halley, his wife, is with him."

Nick showed her the highlights of the resort and then steered her to the tropical garden. Entering it, they found Todd and Halley.

Halley's eyes widened when she saw Shannon and Nick approaching. "Todd," she whispered, "she is just as Adam described, just the way I painted her! I need to have her visit us in NYC so they can meet." She stopped as the pair drew closer.

"Hello, Nick. What's happening?" she asked.

"Halley and Todd, meet Shannon. She helped deliver the twins. She is checking on them today."

Halley quickly asked, "Shannon, can you stay a while? We are soon going to Ti Chi class."

Shannon smiled. "Well, it *is* my day off. Nick, can I join the class?"

"Sure. Go with Halley and Todd."

They entered the Ti Chi room. Shannon slipped into yoga pants taken from her large handbag. Special slippers, available from the resort, were required before taking a floor position. The fifteen clients moved slowly in unison, following the leader's calls: Salutation, Greeting, Carry Ball, Part Wild Horse's Mane, Catch Ball, Stroke Bird's Tail, Draw Out Net, Pull in Net, Crack the Whip, Play the Fiddle, Push the Wall, second Play the Fiddle, Wild Goose Open, Brush Knee, Four Brush Knee, Apparent Closure and Hail Sun.

As the class ended, the leader, Brian, asked them to "keep your eyes shut and concentrate how the body has awakened and the muscles relaxed. Practice in early morning and before bed. Clients with long work hours can add movements at midday to keep the body supple. I will be doing these exercises at the courtyard daily at seven a.m. Anyone can come."

Halley, Todd and Shannon walked back to the resort diner.

Chapter 37

HALLEY ASKED. "TELL ME WHAT YOU SEE AND FEEL ABOUT these paintings, Shannon. I've heard many interpretations."

"Being from Scotland, this one makes me yearn for home. The greens seem alive. The craggy hills and twisty road are right too. Look at the brightness in the summer flowers, so skilfully wound around in just the right places. This next one gives me a strong sense of *déjà vu*. The ocean pushes the rocks at the shore and the bending of the trees shows the wind is strong. That is what I see at my birth home. The colors, too, are genuine to the place!" She laughed. "I have not felt so moved by a painting before!"

"I have a friend at home who needs to meet you, Shannon. He has a painting of you!"

"I never posed for anyone. How could it be me?"

"He had a dream that kept repeating, and you are the beauty he described."

"Where is home, Halley?"

"First, describe what you see in the other paintings."

"Look at this one—it calls to us with the hidden faces in the clouds, trees, water. This artist has amazing power."

"This artist has prayers and blessings placed on each work. Look at the next one. "

"Do you see a woman holding a baby? There is a wolf head gazing on them. Over here are shamrocks with a fox and its young. Gazing on them is a man's face. Do you know the artist, Halley? It is clever artistry. Very emotional! In a good way. I'd like to meet A.L. Waters. The paintings on the other wall held remind me so much of my home in Scotland. I was moved by them too!"

"Shannon, I am from the Big Apple, New York City. Here is my e-mail. Please plan to visit soon. You can stay with us. Todd and I return in a week. Could I have your e-mail?

"You are very spiritual. I'd like to visit you both. Here is my card."

Chapter 38

SCOTT HAYES WAS IN THE HOT TUB WITH SHEILA HOLMES, drinking champagne and eating grapes and strawberries. "Have you decided which time of day is best to share with me, Sheila? I can only hope your day is not totally filled with other plans."

"You won't be tracking fraud, identity theft, crime or domestic violence?"

"This is my long-awaited holiday time. No way will I be coerced back to work!"

"We could catch some rays so I don't look pale. You can rub oil on me."

"Why are we waiting? I'm at your service."

"I'll meet you at the pool then with my oils, handsome!" She lightly kissed Scott and left.

Scott thought to collect towels, robes and water bottles. How lucky was he to holiday when she came?

Jill was in a meditation session. *Why did I choose a quiet, slow session? Okay, self, I know. I need to learn to debrief myself when the burden is too heavy. Focus now.*

Chan, the leader of the session, asked for feedback.

Jill asked, "In what other ways can a person meditate?"

"Some people find Ti Chi movements relaxing and stress relieving. Others do reiterative singing or speaking, and there are those who use soothing music. The ancients felt it was wise to focus on silence. One's mind is busy with daily living and needs to free itself for part of the day. It takes deep concentration for silence. When reached, the results are very positive."

* * *

At dinner, Scott, Sheila, Shannon and Nick sat at one round table. The conversation was lively; however, Nick was feeling low. Finally he took the bull by the horns and declared, "Help me out here—" only to be interrupted by hands covering his eyes and a voice saying, "I was ordered to arrive here ASAP! What help is needed?" Cora smiled at the other guests, keeping her hands on Nick's eyes. He reached to them and felt the rings on her fingers—not Sasha! Her hands had heated his eyes quickly. He turned to see who it was.

"Cora! Let's have a talk away from here." He rose from the table and, wrapping an arm at her waist, led her outside. He asked, "Did Sasha come with you?"

"No, she is in a relationship with man from Texas. Are you disappointed?"

"Cora, we need to do things together and get to know each other. We can—"

"How did you know I was Cora?"

"Halley and Sasha talked about you and these lovely accounting hands."

"I need food. Perhaps we could go to your home kitchen, Nick?" He turned her and they moved through the gardens as

Cora said, "We were so happy Todd was found and reunited with our sister. How are they healing here?"

"See for yourself—they are dining here." Entering the home they walk into a hall and then the open kitchen, dining and living room. Mike, Trudy, Todd and Halley were on dessert.

"Hello, everyone. Look what came down the road!" Nick laughed. Halley jumped up and hugged Cora. Trudy got her arms around both.

Cora laughed, "I was rushing to get here."

"You must be Cora," said Trudy. "Please sit and have dessert and coffee with us. How was your trip?"

"Good. I had to hurry rearranging my life." Turning, Cora continued, "Halley you specifically—"

"Shush, Cora. Come to the table now." Halley led her to sit her between Nick and herself.

"Hey, Todd. You look stronger now, or is it an illusion?"

Todd laughed as he took her hand and said, "The air is clean and between sessions of swimming and hiking I've been renewing my body and mind. It is good to see you, Cora."

Halley returned with a cold plate of sliced meat and cheese with fresh bread, and another with fruits and lemon cream puffs. Setting these before Cora, she smiled and said, "Refresh and enjoy, Sister!"

Mike remarked, "Cora, I hope you plan a few days here. Autumn is extra bountiful in color. And should you become bored, we have an opening in accounting."

Trudy suggested, "Cora, make time to benefit from the many sessions we have going!"

"I hope to hike in the mornings, then I can do afternoon sessions," Cora stated "I have a competent staff now, so I planned on two weeks here, if rooms are available."

Trudy replied, "We can place you in a room next to Halley. Mike, we need to follow through with Chef George. Now is best as they are on clean-up."

"Let's go, Trudy. See you all in the morning."

Nick had a second helping of dessert, saying, "Scott seems to have a love interest now in Sheila. Halley, did you put out a request for them?"

"Foolish you are, Nick. Scot himself asked for help several times. Back home, my friend Adam described a woman he kept dreaming of. I painted her according to his description and hung the paintings in in his living room. He excitedly called me to say they truly captured her. Shannon looks like the match."

Todd asked, "What's this about Scott and Sheila? They arrived this morning and I never had a chance to speak with him. He usually quickly checks in with us, Halley. Scott told me earlier to find someone like my wife for him. I said they broke the form when Halley was made." He laughed some more, winking at Nick.

Jill heard this as she arrived. "Todd, I just left them in the resort diner eating and conversing, laughing a lot. No worry for us."

Nick said, "Scott helped you and Halley. You've known him longer than I."

Halley suggested, " Maybe Jill can tell us about Sheila. Does she work with you, Jill?"

"Are you guys matchmakers? I could use a man in my life!" Jill laughed. "But my twin, Judy, needs one also! Sheila is our top legal executive and advisor plus a researcher, organizing the staff and the bosses. She has been showing signs of discontent these last two weeks. She loved the outdoors when we came here earlier. We work out in a gym, but it's stuffy and boring.

Let's see, Sheila... She reads detective novels, is a great cook and has First Aid training. As a group we go to the pub every two weeks and enjoy the atmosphere. We like to dance and play darts."

Cora said, "You missed out her family. It has fifth generation detectives. Often they call on Sheila when a stumbling block occurs. Why did Sheila do a different career? Ask her. I know this because one of her brothers travelled with me in Spain last year."

"Okay, I will!" Jill added, "She's had two boyfriends in long relationships. Sadly the first one died in a traffic accident. The other was shot on a hunting trip. After that she quit dating. As a group of girls at work, we rally around, supporting each other. At work we never mention family unless it is a positive remark."

Nick stood and asked Cora to take a walk with him, Halley and Todd.

"Jill, go swimming to lower your energy and then you can practice the meditation learned today. It will impress Chan, and show the other clients why we study."

"I like the way you think, Nick. Perhaps you have taken sessions here?" Jill laughed.

Halley took Cora's hand and led her outside. "Cora, your personality is better for Nick, should you fall for him. You're a gym workaholic and that translates to what Nick does hiking. You're a joker, prankster, great observer, hardworking, good cook, love children, and a general quiet strong friend. Your family of three is close to his. His sister Beth just had twins a couple weeks ago. Either of you could move across the country, without blinking. You are a straight shooter and know how to have fun with a guy. Enjoy your holiday."

"Thanks, Halley. I'll be discreet. Go join Todd."

Chapter 39

SCOTT AND SHEILA WERE SITTING IN THE GAZEBO, CONVERS-
ing about their families and friends. Scott explained, "I have an
older sister, Angie, who has two boys eight and ten years old.
She wed a lawyer and they live in Los Angeles. My parents
moved to be near the grandchildren. Dad is seventy and Mom
sixty-six. I visit them all at Easter, Thanksgiving, and Christmas.
Sheila, did you learn researching at college and working with
the lawyers?"

"Basically, I found it easy to relate to the work. I'm a born an
organizer; my firm recognized this and advanced me quickly. I
easily make woman friends, even in the workforce. Halley give
me some hints about your FBI background, Scott. You seemed
like my family, who have detective careers over five generations.
People who meet Halley soon seem to make more connections.
She was in recovery herself but reached out to give solace to
others. I met her in the resort diner and we talked, baring our
souls. Those paintings in the diner draw the viewer to expose
her/his feelings. You can study one for hours. Did they pur-
chase them locally, do you know?"

"Friends from Seattle, and New York or DC is what I heard. Let's study them in the morning at breakfast. Did you involve yourself with the detectives, searching for clues?"

"When they were stumped, they called for my suggestions. It often helped. Made me proud to help, however it's not what I desire. Have you known Halley and Todd for long?"

"I met Todd at my gym. We've been friends for a couple years. Halley and Todd are soul mates. She was adamant that Todd was alive and needed healing prayers. When he was found, I went to him in the hospital. He stated he saw visions of her praying for him. I believed him. What do you think of that?"

"It is like the government denying UFOs exist. Spirituality holds a mysterious power. My mom often told our family, the Bible states Jesus says ask for help from him and help will come. When my boyfriends were killed, I asked Jesus to help me heal and move forward. Asking daily and several times during the day, eventually I released the pain and matured. Prayer kept me focused on the law work. When I felt lost at home I stopped, centered my thoughts and prayed."

"Do you believe there are psychics, who if asked can help the police find clues?"

"Humans are one on Earth. They each have differing abilities. I've seen a young woman who kept coming to us at the law office to reveal where a body could be found. She had continued visions and was troubled about it. Finally I called the Police Chief to come in and listen to her. I thought having a third person there might induce him to take it seriously. He put men on it, she rode with them and at the spot she indicated they probed and found a child murdered. Yes, I believe."

"The FBI has a research division that checks people who have amazing minds."

"Scott, in our years of marriage, are we still going to discuss things so seriously?" Sheila laughed.

"Do you like pub runs, playing darts and dancing, Sheila?"

"Yes, yes and yes! I heaved a dart once or twice. Where do we do these events? The sooner, the better. I'm game!"

"Come. Let's walk some, then retire. It's eleven, but here with the magic lights it seems earlier."

They joined hands and walked the lighted garden trails. The scents were heavenly.

Chapter 40

NICK AND CORA HAD HIKED TO THE LOOKOUT SPOT WITH the view of the resort. Now they sat in the library, munching snacks and drinking tea and juice. He was still unsure of her motives for advancing on him in the diner, but he had discovered she was unique and interesting. She made him laugh. She had vast knowledge of varied topics he'd introduced. Who would believe, she had a brother that restored automobiles, and even assisted him! Nick needed her to see his Mustang.

Cora felt comfortable with Nick, enjoying his quick conversation twists. She almost topped him on some ideas, then remembered, men did not like to be showed inferior. He was grilling her. *Let's give him a twist.*

"Nick, do you like children? You never mentioned Beth tonight."

Laughing, Nick said, "I set priorities years back. Her twins awakened me. She's younger and I never thought of settling down. Her Phil was away on a deal, making her lonely and complaining. I said no husband wants a nagger and she had better shape up. The Doc never told her twins were expected. Phil was at the delivery and he loved the doubles! He calmed Beth."

"Has she help to take care of them and herself?"

"Two days ago, Phil brought her an assistant. She lives in house. And her friend Mavis in Seattle often comes or calls. Mom and Dad are over the moon for the babies."

"Having babies changes how the mother looks on life. There are some mothers who suffer from depression after baby's birth."

"I'd like to have someone to share my life. She needs to be independent, believe in family, have humour, high self-esteem, be honest and trustworthy, and love me." He points to Cora. "Think you fit the bill?"

"Nick. What are you holding back?"

"Halley revealed that she and Todd felt sparks up their arms, on their first encounter. They were only married eight months when he disappeared. She denied that he was dead, insisted he only needing healing. She prayed for him when I was with her. She's authentic. Todd said they connected immediately."

"Yes I was one of their bridesmaids. I cherish Halley's personality. She does not gossip, is always fair and has great compassion. Her paintings are riveting. I love her!"

The clock chimed midnight. Nick kissed Cora goodnight and they agreed to meet for Tai Chi the next day.

Chapter **41**

JILL HAD RETURNED TO PORTLAND. SHE WAS WISER ABOUT herself now. She could build on her skills learned at the Red Rock. Chan advised her to practice daily, and then check for a leader in Portland who could certify her to teach it. She was energized and looking to meet a gentleman. First she had to convince her twin, Judy, she needed to do the same.

Ten days after Sheila and Scott met, they left the resort and headed to their separate homes. They agreed they were free to date where they lived but would still keep in touch with each other.

Nick and Cora spent time restoring his Mustang. Cora was anxious to see it completed and suggested they tackle it together. In the mornings they did Tai Chi, snacked, then hiked one to two hours. They ate lunch and then moved to the chores of restoration. Evening found them soaking in the hot tub. The evening meal was shared with the resort's guests, receiving good feedback for the resort business.

The completed, gleaming red Mustang was a beaut! It ran smooth and fast. Cora had talked Nick out of a black interior, suggesting instead caramel leather. He appreciated it!

"You surprised me, Cora. Your small frame is deceptive!"

"It's done now, and you won't have to nag your family for free time. The time flew—but I must return to the Big Apple. I already booked my flight for noon tomorrow. It has been a blast, Nick. I'm hungry and am going in to eat. I will just look at the resort paintings again first."

Nick pulled her into his body and gave her a long kiss. She responded uneasily. Releasing her, Nick said,

"Okay, let's eat. I can give you a Mustang ride to the airport."

He called the chef to set up a hearty meal for two and deliver it to home base.

*　*　*

Cora was in the diner, studying the paintings by A.L. Waters. Of course she knew the artist! She could easily discern the hidden faces; however Nick did not. She moved to the ones by A.J. Swan. These also had movement, good composition, great color and texture, but were not as riveting as Waters' paintings. *Maybe I'm biased, knowing A.L. so long,* she thought. Alice, she remembered Halley describing, was only five foot tall but packed with humour. Halley had said she wore bright interesting clothes and was a great cook. She should call Alice and see if she was showing her art in galleries.

She turned and nearly bumped into another guest who had been behind her. He caught her arm and spoke softly, "I saw you riveted by this painting and had to look myself. What did you see in it?"

"Sir! Look at the fabulous colors used, the textures, and a composition that begs you to linger and view the outdoors. The movement in the trees, grass and flowers shows it's a breezy day. Do you see?"

"I was more inclined to the other wall. I have not studied these yet. Walk with me to the Waters paintings. This second one reflects the colors in my home and drew me in. Can you see hidden treasures in it?"

Nick called, " Come Cora, lunch is ready."

"Sorry, I must leave," Cora apologized. "My partner is waiting."

He took Cora to the home dining room. They ate quietly and comfortably together.

"Nick, let's leave at eleven. I can get in a run before that and be packed and ready."

"That works with my unscheduled free day. I'll see you then."

She quickly headed to her quarters, glad that a kiss was avoided. *I must explain to Halley what happened before I leave.* Showered and packed for her journey, she slipped into bed and was soon sleeping deeply.

* * *

Todd and Halley were finishing their evening meal when Nick came to the resort diner. He looked happy. "Friends, you gave me a shake when Cora advanced on me. Now the Mustang has its glow refreshed, thanks to Cora. Her brothers taught her well. She told me what parts needed ordering before I found out myself. It was a big time saver! The Mustang ran smooth and powerful on our test run." He pulled out a chair and sat beside them. "We came in to eat a while back and while I ordered, she wanted to take another look at the resort paintings. A man came in and tried moving in on her. She dismissed him handily. What a day!" He shook his head regretfully. "I tried, Halley, but we did not have the spark. Man, she is great at restoring cars, though!"

Todd explained to Nick what he and Halley had done all day. "I wrote some suggestions gleaned from other guests and ourselves. Slip them into your pocket. Shannon has gone back to Seattle. Halley has Shannon skyping with a hospital administrator in New York, seeking a position for herself."

Chapter **42**

TWELVE DAYS HAD GONE BY. AFTER RUNNING THREE MILES, Halley and Todd showered, then packed for the journey home. The Red Rock visit had been a wonderful healing time for both.

Trudy had breakfast laid out. A fluffy kale omelette, grilled fish, cinnamon buns, rice casserole, fresh fruit and juices.

"Have I learned from you Halley, how to do a better breakfast?"

"It is wonderful, Trudy. Our short time together was packed with power. Thank you for having us."

"I like this breakfast. It is nutritious and easy on the digestion," Todd remarked. "Trudy, what gave you the inspiration for this healing retreat?"

"People need beautiful surroundings as they seek healing. I was in nursing and Mike was in banking. After twenty years of marriage, I saw this need and we searched for the right combination to use before building the resort. The chefs and class instructors are eager to be here. The dream hoops at the stairwell attest to the need. It is an ever-changing adventure! I love the work."

Halley patted Trudy's shoulder. "Nursing and this work is coordinated. Work done with love is really worship of God. It is a service that exceptional people do with heart and soul."

Todd adds, "I had a wonderful time here, Trudy. Thank you. Today Halley and I leave for home. We will keep in touch."

Chapter **43**

SEATED IN THE PLANE WITH HIS LEGS STRETCHED FORWARD, Todd was soon asleep. Halley meditated for thirty minutes. She rose and headed to the restroom, passing young twin girls seated alone. On returning, Halley slipped into the empty seat to talk with them.

"Hello, girls. I'm Halley. Have you done much flying?"

"We are twins. I'm Tessa and this is my sister, Tina. It is our first plane ride. I'm nervous. Tina is hungry. Can we get food?"

"I have some granola bars and water and will share with you. Here you go, girls. I would love to have twins. We don't have children yet. How far are you travelling?"

"We are not sure."

"Show me your plane tickets and we will find out."

Tessa reached into her backpack, pulled out the ticket and handed it over.

"Just like us, you stop at Chicago. Have you other planes to board?" Halley noted the surname Taylor.

"That is the only ticket we have, Halley. Can you help us?"

"Where is your family, Tessa?"

"My mom is very ill and our dad died two years ago. Mom put on us on the plane and said a lady with reddish hair would help us. There are no other relatives."

Halley hugged her Tessa and reached over to hug Tina. "I will help you. Let me talk with the stewardess."

She questioned the stewardess: how were these girls boarded without adults?

The reply was, "We have youngsters travelling alone frequently."

"Do you have sandwiches, nuts, fruit and juice I can buy for them?"

"Certainly, I'll take those to them."

Returning, Halley addressed the girls. "You're in luck; the stewardess will bring you some food. Tina, come forward with me and meet my husband, Todd."

Tina asked, "Does he like kids?"

"Yes he loves kids. Oh my. He still sleeps. Tina, he is a kind man. Was your dad a kind man?"

"Yes. I miss him. He was a policeman. He took good care of us."

"Todd and I will take good care of you on the flight. Let's go back and get food."

"I like the sandwich, said Tessa shyly. "Thank you, Halley. Here, Tina, have half of mine."

"Tessa, what was your dad's name and your mom's?" asked Halley.

"Lynn and Ross."

"Did your mom work outside your home?"

"She is a math teacher at our school."

"What is the name of your school? Where is it?"

"Whispering Hills, in Seattle."

"Girls what age are you?"

"Ten. We have a birthday September 9."

"My birthday is September 19. Tessa, go to the front and sit with my Todd. Drat I need the restroom." In the small enclosed place, Halley phoned Scott Hayes and relayed what she had learned from the twins. She wanted him to clear the way for them to adopt, after contacting the mom.

Tessa reached the seats where Tina had gone earlier and found a man looking out the window.

Before sitting she called, "Todd?" He turned and smiled. "Hi."

"Hello, Todd. Halley sent me to you. My name is Tessa, my twin sister is Tina. We were sitting alone and Halley came to our rescue. She said you are kind and you will help take care of us. Do you agree?"

"Certainly if, everything checks out."

"What do you mean?"

"Tessa, I am a lawyer. We have procedures to follow to make sure things are done properly."

"Poof! I knew it was too good to be true." She became teary eyed.

"Hey, it's okay! Here, sit down with me. Where are Dad and Mom?"

"I told Halley. Dad was a policeman. He died two years ago. Mom is very ill. She put us on the plane and said someone with reddish hair would help us. We don't have other relatives."

"Don't be frightened. We will care for you until we have all the information. Tell me about your school."

"Tina and I are good in school. Mom said we had two more years to decide our future. Tina is very good in Places, Music and Art. I am good in Math and Science. Whatever I choose, it will be to help mankind."

"What kind of crazy things happen with schoolmates?"

Tessa smiled. "We had a canoe trip and the kids purposely tipped it. The teacher did not panic. He shouted, 'Learn from this!' I was glad it was a hot day." She giggled.

"Learn by error, huh? Halley is a painter and she also takes beautiful photos. Besides canoeing, what other sports interest you?"

"I watch people paragliding and would like to do it! I like softball, soccer and riding horses. I would like to learn tennis and to dance. Do you do sports, Todd?"

"I love dancing with my Halley. I play tennis, basketball, bowling, and sometimes baseball. And we both ride horses. Is there gymnastics at your school?"

"That's an indoor sport. Not my thing!"

"You could do it outdoors!" He chuckles. "Do you have any questions for me, Tessa?"

"You have grey hair, trembling hands and do not smile."

"You have me figured out! You with the short hair, tiny eyes and frown."

"You figured me out!"

"What movies do you like? What music?"

"*Harry Potter*. Mom plays guitar and bluegrass music. I like it."

"I could sleep a bit more. Are you sleepy?"

A sudden yawn overtakes her. She curled up in her seat and closed her eyes.

Meanwhile, Halley asks, "Tina ,what are your likes and dislikes?"

"I don't like milk. Yogurt is good. Cereal in boxes is okay if I can eat it dry. I eat hot dogs, no-gluten bread, fruits, vegetables, rice and beans. I like shorts and T-shirts, school and my friends there. I draw. I *don't* like not having Mom with us."

"Remember Tina, my Todd and I will care for you and Tessa. We just need to sort it out. Do you do sports?"

"Sure. We did a school canoe trip. We ride bicycles, play dodge ball, soccer, skipping tricks, and I love swimming."

"I do photography and painting. I hike and do the sports you like. What books do you read?"

"I'm improving my school reading. I really like drawing though."

"I bet you like movies. Which ones are best?" Halley tickled her and squealing laughter was released.

Gulping air, Tina replies, "*Harry Potter*, *Frozen* and ones with animals Disney makes. Halley, you will be a good Mom for us. I want to sleep now."

" Okay. Relax and sleep."

*   *   *

Arriving at Chicago, Todd and Halley walked holding the twins' hands between them. They stopped to get plane tickets for the twins to NYC. With an hour waiting time, they head to a restaurant for food.

"Halley can we have pita burgers?"

"I think we can all have pita burgers." Todd winked at the girls and they giggled.

Tina boldly looked at Todd, saying, "Could we add one order fries for Tessa and me?"

"Good idea." He turned to the waitress and placed the orders.

E.P. STASZ

"Girls, did your mom put papers in your backpacks?" It bothered Halley that their mom seemed to have described her to the twins but hadn't made firm plans for them.

She watched them reach into their backpacks and heard a rattle that made Tessa exclaim, "I have an envelope that I never put in!" Lifting out the thick brown envelope, she turned it over and said, "Look Halley, your name is on it!" She handed it over.

The food arrived and the waitress added a plate with fresh mixed vegetables.

"Our manager saw the twins and made the no-cost addition. Enjoy!"

The twins turned their attention to the food. Todd cut their large pita burgers in half to make them easier to handle.

The manager, Bill Barr, came over. "Hi, good to see you, Todd. You made good investments for me and now I have this. Thank you. How have you been?"

"Bill, we are good. I'm glad of your success. How is your family?"

"Our boy is in college studying law and our girl is a nurse. My wife has a hair salon. Your meal is on the house. You've made us very fortunate."

The waitress hurried to them and asked Bill to see to a problem in the kitchen.

"Thank you, Bill," Todd and the twins called out.

Halley was busy shuffling through the envelope material: birth certificates, school reports from grades one to five, the twins' medical records, an address book, class lists and bank information. A marriage certificate and their father's death certificate. There was also a letter addressed to Halley with Scotch tape over the seal. *Hopefully this will clear the way to keeping the twins.* She returned her attention to her "family."

She looked at Todd, who was engrossed in watching the twins. She said, "Pretty remarkable girls."

Todd beamed at her. "Remarkable wife, too! Is there sufficient information in the envelope?"

"Earlier I called Scott to look into it. The envelope has a lot of information to help get them into school, and a letter to me. I haven't opened it yet—we can study it all at home." Turning to the twins, she said, "Do twins eat the same things?"

"Not likely," scoffed Tina. "I like vinegar on fries but Tessa must have ketchup."

"You can eat my fries, Tina, because I prefer vinegar too. Is the pita burger good?"

"Yum, yum, yum!" giggling girls reply.

She glanced again at Todd and found him watching her. He slowly grinned, saying, "Love, we can do it. I'm already smitten." He chuckled.

She stood and kissed him. "Love, we can— "

Tessa interrupted, "Hey, you guys. You act like Mom and Dad used to!"

"That's love, little girl." He bent and kissed her cheek, then leaned farter to do the same to Tina. "Let's do some walking while we wait. We'll see what there is to see andkeep our body joints oiled. Everyone ready?"

"Yes," they reply.

Chapter 44

THE TAXI STOPPED AT THEIR HOME AND THE TWINS exclaimed in excitement.

"It's big!"

"Maybe a castle?"

Halley laughed and stated, "Castles are cold but our home is warm. Pay attention to the flowers and trees. Smell them up close."

Todd chuckled, "Let them fall in love with it. I'll open up the house."

"This beautiful tree is for us, Tina. Join my hands—can we meet?"

Tina shouted, "Hurry, Halley, join us so we can meet!"

Laughing, she did as requested. With her hands on their shoulders, she said, "Girls, it is a very old oak. Todd will show you how to climb the branches."

"He's waiting on the steps for us." Tessa started running, with Tina close behind. They ran, paying no attention to the pots on the steps holding masses of scented and colorful flowers. Todd felt his heart fill as they joined him, grabbing his hands.

"Place your packs on this bench and be patient."

He picked up Tina and carried her over the threshold, then did the same with Tessa. As Halley came, he picked her up and carried her inside. He embraced her, saying, "We are home, my love, and we start a new life."

She replied. "Yes. My husband Todd!"

Halley turned to the girls. "Bring your packs in and place them by the stairs. Leave your shoes on this rack. It will take awhile to learn about our home. When they were ready, she said, "From here we can see the kitchen, and come this other way we find a restroom, a library, Todd's office and a den. The garage is through that door. Now we go upstairs!"

Tina and Tessa looked at each other and Tina said, "It's big like a castle." They giggled as they followed Halley upstairs.

"Here is a music room, restroom, computer area, two bedrooms and the master bedroom. On this other side is the laundry room, three bedrooms and a playroom. The bedrooms have a Jack and Jill bath. What would you girls like, bunk beds or twin beds in the same room, or separate rooms?"

"Halley, you decide for us," Tessa requested.

"I think we'll put you in one room with twin beds. Why? You're in a new place and it will be comforting to be together. You should be close to my bedroom so you can easily find us. If our door is locked, pound on the door. Then wait."

"It is a beautiful place," said Tina. "Our house was smaller. Halley, do you have dogs or cats?"

"No, we don't. As we get to know each other, we can make changes. Look up here. It is called a vaulted ceiling, and below you see our living room. Follow me down to the kitchen."

In the kitchen, Todd had milkshakes made for the twins and tea for the adults.

"Todd, what did you use for milk?"

"I did not chance it and used nut silk. We also have fruit, cheese, ham and gluten-free biscuits. There was a note on the pizza box. It was made with no-gluten flour."

"Girls, the shakes are not milk. The rest is safe too."

"Halley and Todd, we like this home. After snacks, can we sleep?"

"Of course. You must be tired after the long plane rides. I'll get a room ready for you."

"I will help, Halley," said Todd.

"Halley, our Sasha has—" he found her standing in the bedroom next to theirs, silently weeping.

The twin beds were dressed in purple with fluffy pillows in yellow and purple. On the beds were yellow nightgowns. Slippers rested on the floor by the beds. There were fresh flowers on each bed table.

"Are you okay, my wife? Sasha left a note downstairs. Cora helped her do this for us. Let's bring the girls up, love." He took her hand.

"Wait, Todd, our friends must have done the bathroom too."

There were fresh flowers on the vanity, stacked yellow towels, pale purple bathrobes, glasses holding toothbrushes still wrapped in plastic, two sets of hand mirrors, each with brushes and combs, and two trays holding groups of yellow and purple candles.

Downstairs, the girls sat in the living room, looking at everything.

"You can explore tomorrow, girls. Come up to take a shower now and then sleep." Halley winked at Todd.

Reaching the bathroom, the girls gasped at the sight of everything set out for them.

"Our friends came to dress up a room for you beautiful twins. These bathroom hampers are for the soiled clothes. Do you need help showering? These robes are for you, and here are towels to dry off with. We can wash your hair tomorrow. Tonight, I will help do one braid. See you soon."

Halley rushed to her room to find scrunchies for the braids.

* * *

"I really like my nightgown. Thank you, Halley." Tina laughed and spun in a circle. "Look how it swirls."

Tessa spun too and exclaimed, "It's soft and pretty!" She hugged Halley and Tina joined in.

The braids were done when Todd called to them, "Be on the beds and I will tell you a story." The twins giggled and scramble up one bed.

Todd came in and said, "Looking good. We can start!" He wiggled between them and wrapped an arm around each twin's shoulder. The girls couldn't stop giggling.

"There was once a Hobbit man and a Fairy woman who walked the same area of sandy beach, but at different times. He had a wiggly high red hat and wore a yellow shirt and baggy blue pants. He had yellow high boots with upturned toes. Once the man saw the Fairy and checked his watch. It was eight p.m. He was careful to study what she did and not be noticed. She had a camera and snapped shots. Another time she sketched. She was slim, with red hair and a flowing dress of pale blue-green. A large white dog came from the forest and stood by her. She placed a hand on the dog's head. The Hobbit and the Fairy saw deer come to drink at the water bubbling between boulders streaming to the sand. He could not clearly see her face. He was interested in her and made a note to bring binoculars next time he came. He worked hard for the next week, and many days later returned to the beach with binoculars. He viewed the coyotes that came to drink the bubbling water and the seagulls screeching over the waves, but no woman. He waited and waited. Disappointed, he returned to his small forest home and studied the picture inside while soothing music played."

Halley whispered, "They are asleep, love. Let them stay together in the one bed for tonight. I'll turn their lamp to dim."

Chapter 45

TODD AND HALLEY SAT DOWN TO READ ALL THE INFORMA-
tion in the twins' envelope.

Todd questioned, "Why did the mom choose you, Halley? This information is mostly on the twins." He sifted through insurance policies, photos of the family, and adoption papers.

"Lynn attended bereavement sessions at Red Rock." Halley passed Todd a couple of photos. "I know by these photos that I talked with her there. She must have asked others about me. Read her letter."

July 29

Dearest Halley,

I am mom, Lynn Joy Taylor, to beautiful twins, Tina and Tessa. I'm a teacher; however in June I was diagnosed with a terminal illness. Soon I will join my late husband, Ross. We were both only children to parents that have already passed.

In the Red Rock bereavement sessions, I sought a solution for leaving my girls. I saw you, Halley—a person hiding pain inside yet displaying to others her smiles, compassion, courage, and positive attitude. Besides, you have strong spirituality!

You and yours need my twins to bring back love and joy. After this decision, my shoulders are held straighter and my heart is at ease.

When I pass, the twins should not come. Have them remember us by our albums. Let them know we will always love them.

Love to you and yours, Lynn.

P.S. Bob and Sam know me too.

"Halley, we need to learn from Lynn's doctors what her chances really are. The adoption papers need to be signed by both partners and witnessed and dated. I wonder if she made a will expressing her wish that the twins come to us? Adoption means name changes usually. Is that what Lynn really wants? We better have the FBI check these questions."

"Should we contact Scott to look into all this? "

"I don't mean to shirk our duty, sweetheart. The twins need to be settled. Tina said she misses her mom, and I'm sure Tessa does too. Couldn't Lynn talk by phone to them? Couldn't they try writing letters to each other? Or even use a tape recorder? It would help all three!"

"Let's list all our queries before we contact Scott. I really want the doctor's report first. Another question, where are all the albums she referred to, framed pictures and the twins' favourite clothes and sports gear?"

Scott sighed and shrugged. "It's a lot to sort out. Halley, let's go to bed now. Place these in my office and we will handle it in the morning."

Chapter 46

SLOWLY A FEATHER WAS BEING BRUSHED OVER HALLEY'S face. She still slept, but her hand pushedacross her face. Giggles got louder, waking her up.

"Ah ha! What are you angels doing?"

"Todd said you must come and have breakfast with us. If you don't get up we are to jump on you!"

Halley squealed, "No! No! I'll be hurt if you jump!" She swung her legs to the floor, bringing the top blanket with her and covering her head. She moaned, "This ghost is gonna get you! Gonna get you! Get you!"

The squealing twins ran to the door, saying, "Come and get us! Ha ha ha!"

They ran downstairs, yelling for Todd to save them. Todd grabbed the girls as they came into the kitchen and showed them where to hide and scare Halley with a loud BOO as soon as she passed by them. "Be quiet, so she doesn't spot you first."

Halley soon appeared and jerked sideways when loud BOOs come from behind her. "We got the ghost. We got the ghost!" the twins sang and grabbed her hands to take her to Todd.

Todd embraced Halley. "I hope my lovely wife still loves me!" he whispered in her ear. Releasing her, he found the girls already seated at the table. The prepared breakfast waited for them: toast, scrambled eggs, bacon, mixed fruits, and juices. Filling two cups with coffee, the adults joined the girls.

Halley said a Baha'i prayer:

"O Thou kind Lord! These lovely children are the handiwork of the fingers of Thy might and wondrous signs of Thy greatness. O God! Protect these children, graciously assist them to be educated and enable them to render service to the world of humanity. O God! These children are pearls, cause them to be nurtured within the shell of Thy loving kindness. Thou art the Bountiful, the All-Loving.
—'Abdu'l-Baha'

"Halley, Thank you for the lovely prayer. You make us feel important," Tessa remarked.

"Twins, I'll be happy to teach more prayers. Now we eat, then plan our day. This ghost needs lots of food to survive the pranks you play! Did you give Todd advice about the food you don't eat?"

"We did., but he already knew about it. An Angel told him last night." Tina winked at Todd. "And he had our clothes ready this morning. Thank you."

"Halley, my love. These twins avoid milk and gluten, love to ride bikes and play soccer."

"Tessa and Tina, I hope you will avoid too much sugary food as well. When we grocery shop, we read the food labels to help us with this. Did you have kitchen chores at home?"

Tessa answered, "We know how to use the dishwasher, make microwave popcorn, set the table for meals, and clean the counters, fridge and stove top. We need help to store leftover food." She glanced at her sister and confessed, "Mom tried to get us washing our clothes but we are not too good with it. Tina once washed Mom's dress pants and they got smaller."

Tina joined in, "Tessa washed one of Mom's sweaters and it stretched into a really funny shape. We laughed together. Mom said it could not be fixed. She showed us the label inside. It should have been hand washed."

"You can always ask us first before doing, so we can guide you in keeping all of us in a safe zone!"

The four laughed together.

"T and T and Halley, I need to work in my home office this morning. I'll check in later." Todd excused himself.

*   *   *

The dishwasher was loaded, food stored, and counters washed. Halley and the girls had made the beds and tidied the bathrooms. Laundry was started. It was time to check the yard.

Past the basketball court they entered the yard. Halley had the twins looking left at the mixture of ferns, ornamental kale and low junipers and day lilies. She halted them, saying, "Time to stop and look back at the house."

The twins stood with open mouths, gazing at the tiers of bleeding hearts, fiery red and white petunias, cascading lobelia and geraniums ending on a mass of marigolds. Several minutes later, Tina stammered, " It's magic!"

Tessa sighed, "Yes. A feast of magic!"

"You both have time to take a good look. Turn left, view the whites against the brick wall. The different lilies below, then our vegetable garden." She walked the path, reaching for ripe everbearing strawberries, then apples and handed each girl one. "Taste and enjoy!" She gestured to their water feature. "Waterfalls help hide traffic noise and soothe the listener. Those are Russian olive trees behind it. Turning left, we have a rock garden, displaying creeping bell flower, bearded tongue, alpine asters, pinks, moss phlox, and sedum. Go ahead, wander about and smell the blooms."

Chapter **47**

A DELIVERY VAN PULLED INTO THE DRIVEWAY AND PARKED BY the garage. Todd came out to meet the driver, and soon several boxes were placed by the vehicles in the garage. Returning to the kitchen, he checked through the windows for his family. They were laughing and smelling the beautiful garden Halley and he had made. He gave a quick prayer of thanks: "Life is renewing for us after the chaos. I must treasure each gift I've received. Lord, help me be strong and true and worthy of their love."

Another delivery van rolled into the driveway. The driver had labelled boxes. Todd realized they were sent from Seattle. The garage became storage again! He checked over the labels, then went out to shoot baskets.

"Todd! Todd! The garden is awesome!" Tina and Tessa were shouting with excitement. They looked at each other and together asked, "Can we play basketball with you?"

"My, my. One voice from two people. You are talented!" Halley came to him and hugged tightly. Releasing him, she grabbed the ball and passed it to Tessa. Squeals and shouts ensued.

Out of breath, Tina exclaimed, "We little people need the net lower!"

"Enough ball tossing. Come to the garage, we had some boxes arrive."

Halley asked, "Do we need a water taste first, girls?"

"Yes, please."

Exhausted from the basketball, they entered the garage. Todd instructed, "Girls, I think you should open the boxes together. Start here."

The twins scrambled to pull at the box flaps.

"These are the books Mom arranged for us to show you," said Tessa.

"We will look through them together later, in the den. Open this next one."

Tina shouted, "It's our games! We had lots of fun playing them."

"Halley and Todd, this next box holds the school awards we won. Dad and Mom were proud of us."

"These are our gym and beach shoes."

"Here are our family photos. This is wonderful. You can see us happy together."

"Girls, it is comforting to have these home treasures," said Todd. "The other boxes say clothes, except this one."

The twins opened the small box together. "Ohhhh. We never had this before!" Tina looked at Tessa in wonder. "Look, Sis, it is a redhead fairy in a blue-green dress. Wow! Todd, you told us a story about her."

"I sure did. Now let's take the games, photos and albums and look through them in the den."

Epilogue

THE SCHOOL BUS DOOR OPENED AND OUT RAN TINA, TESSA and Lucy, Fred Nader's granddaughter. In a week it would be Christmas. Halley had snacks ready for the girls. They acted like sisters and were very active. After snacks, they would toss basketballs at the outside net. Tina's reading and drawings were steadily improving. Tessa and Lucy were learning camera compositions. School was easy for them. Halley challenged them with math problems, age relationship issues, and making art sketches. She cooked with them, hoping they learned the value of nutrition and presentation. Todd had them discussing how to handle problems and using logic and critical thought to present a good outcome.

Halley was three months pregnant. She had switched from painting with oils to acrylics for the baby's safety. She kept in touch with Andrea in Baltimore and her brother, S.S. Kelly. Cora often went with her to visit them. The twins adored his barn cats and admired his horses.

Todd had his own law office. He had been retained by three new companies and his business had quickly mushroomed. He and Halley played tennis at the Chase Club. Often they had new partners to play.

The twins had adjusted to their new family. Lucy had joined them after Fred convinced the couple that she needed "young parents' guidance and stamina, besides the joy of sisters." They were a united happy, loving family.

Halley and Todd felt very blessed and thankful for the gift of love. Halley now knew why her spirit had been moved to paint so many girls' faces.

With Fred Nader's team, the couple funded the building of a shelter for pregnant unwed young girls. Sam and Bob set up funding for workers, maintenance, and schooling for those staying in the shelter. They often visited Halley and Todd's family.

Stephanie was working in a top New York hospital. Sasha had won second in hairdressing competitions. She was grateful for her successful new career. Scott had renewed his romance with Sheila. She now worked with Manhattan's Casey & Stevens Law Firm.

Lynn had accepted Todd's plea and telephoned her twins every two days. When she weakened too much, she used a laptop computer for all the things left unsaid. She was most grateful to Bob and Sam for suggesting that Halley would be a super mom. The Yorks had placed Lynn into a Red Rock session on bereavement with Halley. In mid-August, they helped sell her home and buy investments for the twins. Lynn's lawyer had her write a will that gave guardianship of her twins to Halley Coleman and Todd Denver. Her doctor congratulated her on placing her affairs in order.

Todd had made videos of his home, garden and family and sent them to Lynn. He had the twins give regular updates on video. These made Lynn's heart overflow. She was viewing them as she passed to God. Sam and Bob were holding her hands. They had arranged for her late September funeral and "Celebration of Life."

> *Love is patient; love is kind; love is not envious or*
> *boastful or arrogant or rude.*
> *It does not insist on its own way; it is not irritable*
> *or resentful;*
> *it does not rejoice in wrongdoing but rejoices in*
> *the truth.*
> *It bears all things, believes all things, endures*
> *all things.*
> *Love never ends....*
> *And now faith, hope, and love abide; and the*
> *greatest of these is love.*
> – 1 CORINTHIANS 13

– THE END –